The Enemy You Know

Denny Heck

The Enemy You Know

A Jess Stevens Mystery

DENNY HECK

Library of Congress Number: 2002094298
ISBN: Hardcover   1-4010-7324-7
         Softcover   1-4010-7323-9

This is a work of fiction. Names, characters, places and incidents either are the product of the author's imagination or are used fictitiously, and any resemblance to any actual persons, living or dead, events, or locales is entirely coincidental.

This book was printed in the United States of America.

To order additional copies of this book, contact:
Xlibris Corporation
1-888-795-4274
www.Xlibris.com
Orders@Xlibris.com

16355-HECK

Dedication

To Paula Fruci Heck, my Sacco, and to the rest
of the Frucis

ACKNOWLEDGEMENTS

There are far too many people to thank individually for their assistance in this undertaking. A few, however, bear mention. My thanks to Doctors Silverman and Nevitt for the critical help in some basic forensic science issues. I especially thank Detective Bill Hanson, retired, Washington State Patrol. One of Bill's cases served as the inspiration for much of this story and he was a constant source of invaluable law enforcement insight. To him and others, I am deeply indebted for helping me have the most fun of my life.

"Better the devil you know than the devil you don't know ... "

Anthony Trollope, *Barchester Towers* (1857)

CHAPTER ONE

Even the most extraordinary days begin in the most ordinary ways. Jess Stevens would learn that today as the cool, cool air of the early August morning slowly gave way to broiling heat.

Their feet swiftly padded across the pavement in irregular rhythm broken only by the occasional crunching of gravel that had accumulated on the roadside.

The two joggers – runners, really, since they were pacing themselves at eight minute miles – made their way along the North Shore Road in the early morning. Their relationship was full of rituals and this was one of them, a pre-dawn run. He hated running but she made him do it. He much preferred his exercise in some form that had purpose such as bicycle riding (for the scenery) or basketball (for the competition).

"My legs are too short," he protested nearly every day.

"You don't know short," she answered. "Try my legs on, you big baby."

They were a study in contrast. He stood six feet exactly while she stretched to reach five feet. "I'm five six," she told her students with a straight face. "On the inside."

On the outside she was an attractive woman with the swarthy coloring of her Italian ancestors. But her eyes were a dark blue and her features were fine. "The Hun invasions of northern Italy," she would explain. Her most striking feature was her tiny body. She weighed barely a hundred pounds and from a distance, especially when she wore a hat, she looked like a teenager. The hat concealed the graying streaks in her dark brown hair.

Her husband was blonde with a slightly receding hairline. But he possessed none of the tell-tale gray of middle age. His eyes were hazel. He wasn't handsome or even noticeable. Not that he was unpleasant looking at all; he wasn't. But there was nothing distinctive about his face or his features except when you talked to him. Then his eye contact was direct and compelling, giving one a sense of his complete concentration and, by implication, caring.

Her body was striking in its compactness; his was so average as to be nondescript. For as much as he ran – five times a week or as often as she made him – he wasn't as lithe as most runners. He wasn't thin and he wasn't particularly muscular for 180 pounds. Just average.

Their feet continued the padded cadence.

Her strides were shorter but more frequent than his so that they ran perfectly abreast of one another. She could easily outrun him in a long race but he never tempted fate with the challenge. As competitive as he was, he was not stupid.

They had three primary routes, each of a different length. Today he begged for mercy in the form of the short course, only two and a half miles. It suited her, after winning other concessions, because she said she wanted to be at school early. For her, that meant by seven AM. It was another way in which they contrasted. Her biological clock was in rhythm in the early hours; his reached its peak late into the night. And it was another reason he hated to run. "If only we could do this in the evening," he whined halfheartedly. They tried and he just invented other complaints and so she forced him back to mornings.

Their taste in fashion was different as well. She had some; he didn't. She wasn't fussy and didn't put much effort into it. It just came naturally, that sense of taste and color. Her diminutive shape also lent itself to wearing clothes that looked elegant and tasteful. Today she had on a tee shirt, something she rarely wore. It was a gift from him and had several rabbits on it and a play on words about another gray hare.

"I'll get the paper," he said out of breath and bent over with his hands on his knees as they arrived back at the driveway to their new home, "and be up in a minute." She nodded and entered the garage as he extracted the Spokesman Review, or the Daily Mistake as he liked to think of it, from the paper box and pulled out the sports section. He looked forward to the leisurely consumption of the news after her departure but he could not wait for the box score of yesterday's Seattle Mariners game. Thanks to a beefed up pitching staff, he had been pleased more often than disappointed lately.

"Sacco," he yelled up the stairs once inside. "Do you have time for a quick bite and coffee?"

"Sure, Gumbah," she responded, using the slang term of endearment that she had long ago permanently substituted for his name.

Her maiden name was Marianina Sacco although everyone who knew her at all simply called her Sacco. He also called her "paisan", the shortened version of "paisano." It meant fellow countryman in Italian.

After making the coffee, he bounded up the steps two at a time.

The entire second floor was their bedroom with its massive walk-in closets and huge bathroom. A giant bed sat against the north wall and faced south with a view of

Loon Lake through the floor to ceiling glass. The water's edge was steps away, visible through a curtain of Ponderosa pines that provided partial privacy to the house.

She lay naked on the bed on her side and purred teasingly when his head popped through the floor.

"I thought you wanted to be at work by seven?" he asked with a grin from ear to ear as he approached the bed.

She raised her hand out to him. "I haven't had enough aerobic exercise yet." There was no mistaking her intent.

He slowly undressed, savoring the sight of her and his own anticipation and joined her in bed where they made love without hurry as though this morning tryst were the beginning of a stolen holiday. Sex between them was a source of enormous mutual satisfaction and important intimacy and always had been. For him, the mere sight of her small and tight body aroused both desire and tenderness, and today was no different.

Afterwards he stroked her softly on the small of her back where tiny beads of sweat appeared as a result of the second workout. They lay on the bed, spent, and he secretly wished she would turn to him and say, "I think I'll stay home today." But he knew she wouldn't, her sense of responsibility too firm. She gave him a gentle look of warning that hinted she would need to be moving soon. He kissed her softly on the lips and then on the forehead and said, "Come on. Get out from underfoot here. Don't think I can just lie around all day in bed with the likes of you."

Sacco did wonder what he did at home alone all day in the solitude of his thoughts now that he had finished supervising the construction of their home.

He had no experience in construction. Until last February, when he precipitously decided to resign his position and build the house on the lake, any small repairs that needed doing around their former home were either hired done or done by Sacco. Once, he assembled a set of storage shelves for the garage. The 30-minute job lasted several hours and the next day Sacco presented him with a clever, mock trophy inscribed "Most Exceeded Natural Ability Award."

This new home on the lake was different; it was perfect and it was his. He even designed it with help from a book of floor plans. And he acted as his own general contractor, often driving his subcontractors to distraction by simultaneously directing them and asking them questions about everything. They would privately joke to one another that it would pay them to reduce their charges if he would just go find something else to do.

Building the home was an intense passion that occupied him totally. During construction he lived in a small travel trailer that he left early in the morning and only returned to late at night. The hardest part was the separation from Sacco but he had insisted she finish the school year on the other side of the state. Every weekend she made the long trip to the lake and every night he called her.

She worried about his state of mind, and was only partly reassured by his passionate focus on the job of building the house. Now she worried because the house was complete, every last detail having been completed two weeks ago. "What would give him purpose now?" she wondered to herself.

"Up and at 'em." she said bouncing out of bed.

They showered together, just as they had almost every morning of their nearly twenty years of marriage. It was a ritual that started as sexual playfulness but had long since become the time during which they talked the best. The steam opened their pores and their mouths.

When they were finished and dressed, he hurried

downstairs to complete the light breakfast preparations while she concluded what she called her "ablutions." Sacco did her makeup as effortlessly and tastefully as she did her dress, and with the same striking result.

"Big plans for the day, Gumbah?" she asked as she stepped through the sliding door onto the main floor deck. She rarely called him by his given name, Jess. When she did, he took it as a sign of seriousness.

"Plan? What's a plan?" he joked. "Retired people don't plan."

"You're not retired. You're on hiatus."

"I am not. I'm on Loon Lake. Hiatus is where the Kennedys' vacation."

They sat down at the expensive outdoor furniture to have morning coffee, grapefruit and toast. Both found that after exercising, they didn't need or want much food.

More ritual: they ate almost every meal outdoors, and spent the time enjoying the view of Loon Lake and listening for the sound of the loons which were beginning to repopulate their namesake. Jess also used the time to quiz Sacco about her new job as principal at the local high school. He thoroughly enjoyed listening to her talk about her day at school even though the students wouldn't be arriving for another week. It reminded him of how they had first met two decades before while teaching in the same building. She had long since become a building administrator while he had gone in a different direction altogether.

Sacco felt lucky when she successfully applied for the job of principal shortly after the prior school year finished. She had never served as a high school principal but the school board members in the small, rural district thought she was a rare find. They also believed it wouldn't hurt to employ someone married to Jess Stevens.

"Off to the salt mines," she said rising. "Will you make sure the maid cleans these dishes?"

"I'll see that I get to it immediately, ma'am."

He walked her to the garage and opened the car door for her. She turned and kissed him on the lips and he held her for a moment in silence and then gave her a departing squeeze.

"Be home early?" he asked.

"Sorry, Gumbah. Administrivia tonight." Jess knew that meant he would have to fend for himself for dinner while Sacco sat around a meeting table and argued inter-scholastic athletic rules with other administrators. She hated that part of her job since it seemed to occupy so much of her time and had so little to do with what was important, at least to her. Before she was hired for her new position, he tried to talk her into "retirement" since they didn't need the salary anymore.

"I'd die if I couldn't be around the kids. What would I do if I didn't get to see them being mugged by their hormones every day?" The real truth was Sacco believed she needed the security of her job, not the financial security – she didn't need to work again as long as she lived – but the security of having something that she was good at and enjoyed doing. Something a little separate from her husband, even though she loved him deeply. She couldn't tell him that right now because he wouldn't understand.

After waving good-bye, Jess returned to the house and immediately began clearing the dishes from the table on the main floor deck. He spent an hour cleaning and picking up the house. Sometimes, he wished they really did have a maid to help with the huge residence, 5,500 square feet on all three floors, but he couldn't justify it even though he could afford it. This morning he concentrated on the main floor, which contained the kitchen, formal dining room, spare bedroom and bath, and huge living room which, like the upstairs bedroom, fronted the lake with all windows. This floor also contained the master controls to the expensive computer system wired throughout the house.

Tomorrow he thought he would attack the basement. It contained another bedroom, the utility room, and a large sitting room. One corner of the latter was his office area with desk and phone. The wall above it was adorned with the many photographs of his prior and more public life. Outside the sliding doors of the basement – again the south wall was almost all glass – was Sacco's favorite part of the house and the only part she had personally insisted upon: the hot tub area. She loved to unwind at the end of the day by sitting naked in the hot tub with Jess, admiring the starry sky. He pretended to mind only a little.

With his chores finished and the house meeting his high standard for neatness, he turned his attention to the balance of the day. He dismissed the prospect of driving up to the Chewelah Golf Course for a round, probably just an excuse for (over) eating lunch at Polanski's Pizza, or hopping on his Klein bike for a spin around the lake. "Something more restful," he thought. And so he went to the bookcase and pulled down a copy of his favorite book for its third reading, *The Name of the Rose* by Umberto Eco. Reading had become habit since the house was done. Jess spent part of every day reading. Some would say it was more an escape for him than an honest attempt at either entertainment or enlightenment.

Several hours later, long after what should have been lunch time, Jess was stirred from his concentration by the jangling of the phone.

"Hey, Jesse," the deep voice on the other end of the phone said. "How's the handicap? And how's my favorite Italian?" He pronounced it "eye-talian" which was a running joke between him and Sacco. She would feign ethnic offense and tell him it was "Italy" not "Eye-taly."

Jess recognized the caller immediately. Even if his

voice wasn't so distinctive, there was only one person who customarily called him Jesse.

"Fine, Governor. She's fine." Jess referred to the man by his title even though they were close personal friends and had been for years. It was a sign of respect for both the office and this man whom he liked and admired. He failed to respond to the inquiry regarding his golf game, however, because he did not want to admit that frequent play had done nothing to improve it.

"I'll tell her you called. But while I am at it, **why** do I tell her you called?" It came out more curt than Jess intended. Close friends though they were, a call from the Governor reminded Jess of the past and that put him slightly on edge.

"Oh, I don't know, Jesse. Just wanted to remind you that I haven't forgotten you. You may be nearly 300 miles from here but I am thinking of you and I am thinking we should talk about more than your golf game." It was a subtle reference to Jess' non-response. The Governor missed very little. "You know, Jesse," the Governor said more seriously, "I could use your help over here."

Jess knew better. The administration was scandal free and running smoothly and the Governor's job approval rating consistently ran high. But he also knew the Governor was smart enough not to ask him to do something specific because it was too soon. And this Governor, no governor, liked to be turned down. "They don't have much experience at it," Jess thought to himself.

Jess didn't know what to say and he let the silence hang a few seconds. The Governor, with his fabled instincts, understood immediately.

"Tell you what, Jesse. I'm working on something over here. It will take a few weeks but it's coming along. I really just wanted to call and ask you to open up your mind to the possibilities during our next conversation. 'Till then, get that handicap down." With that, he hung up, not waiting for the answer he knew he did not want to hear.

The guy is good, Jess admitted to himself. And for all his resistance to any assignment, no matter how important or interesting, Jess found himself unsettled by the conversation. He certainly didn't need the money or the headache but he knew the Governor and he knew what happened when the man set his jaw with determination.

Jess decided to kill two birds with one stone: shake off the effects of the phone call and catch some dinner by jumping in his new blue and white, 18-foot Bayliner and heading for Granite Point, where the kokanee were said to be biting. Later, he would regret his decision.

CHAPTER TWO

Jess turned the ignition of the Bayliner's 175 horsepower V8 engine and felt an instant response. "God, I love that sound," he said to himself as the boat roared to life. Both the boat and the engine were excessive for his uses, but he had indulged himself with the purchase anyway when the house was finished.

The oversized engine was the direct result of his seminal skiing experience several years before. Back then, the difficult part of learning, as with most beginners, was getting up out of the water. He reasoned that if he had a more powerful motor than the sixty horse outboard they were then using, he would learn faster and be a better skier. Sacco told him to drop 20 pounds instead.

"I think this is a young person's sport," he would sputter, spitting the lake water out of his mouth as Sacco circled him in the boat to prepare for another try. He nearly gave up after the time he fell backwards and the lake managed to give him a sort of enema. But he persisted and eventually prevailed. Now, he could slalom on one ski with the most virile of teenagers.

He guided the boat slowly past the ski dock and the water barrels before gunning it toward Granite Point, the small resort to the southeast. Granite Point was a congenial place, one of two resorts on the lake, with public access, a few cabins for rent, a small campground, a swimming area and a tiny store. The best thing about the store was Ben, the cantankerous retiree who worked there and knew more about the fish in Loon Lake than anyone. Jess liked him ever since he overheard him tell the owner, after a perceived slight, to go flour his nuts.

Ben stood over six feet even given a considerable stoop. He was spindly but not frail and walked with a definite hitch. No one knew exactly how old he was and if they asked, he told them "older than dirt." His face was pure leather and could belong to someone in his late sixties or someone in his early eighties. All most people knew about Ben was that he was widowed with no children, retired from the phone company in Spokane, irascible and not someone to begin a conversation with about fish – unless you had time on your hands.

Yesterday afternoon, when Jess had lunch at the small counter at Granite Point, Ben told him the kokanee were active. Jess' taste for the landlocked salmon was an acquired one. He never liked the flavor until Sacco agreed to clean them and cook them. Suddenly, Jess developed a new-found appreciation for the kokanee of Loon, especially pan fried with a little lemon and garlic.

Ben was specific with his instructions, and unforgiving if you didn't follow them exactly: use maggots, which he would be glad to sell you, go about a quarter mile straight out from the store and drop down four or five pulls. If that didn't bring in a couple of 14 or 15 inchers within ten minutes, then he wasn't the man who had caught the state's record mackinaw trout, at 32 pounds, right here in Loon Lake. Ben needed little excuse to remind people of his ancient trophy catch.

Jess took his time getting to his destination so he could enjoy the lake and the surrounding forested hills. Owning property on Loon Lake was no random occurrence.

When Jess and Sacco were newlyweds, they meticulously searched the Northwest for just the right lake, with an affordable vacant lot on which they could vacation and eventually build a retirement home, in just the right location. They began with a preference for the eastern side of the state, even though it meant several hours of driving, primarily because of the more pronounced seasons and the lower rainfall – twenty inches a year versus more than fifty inches on the wetter west side of the Cascade Mountains that divide Washington. They found their locale north of Spokane in southern Stevens County, a name purely coincidental to Jess and Sacco's. They liked to think of it as "their county."

Their county had the distinction of being one of the most beautiful and most poor in the state. Shaped like a long box, it stretches one hundred miles from the Spokane River in the south to the Canadian border in the north. Its western border is made up primarily of the tamed flow of the Grand Coulee Dammed Columbia River and the resulting Roosevelt Lake. Thirty miles to the east, the ridge of the Chewelah Mountains forms a spine protecting the county's flank.

Fewer than 40,000 people sparsely populate the countryside and many small towns, and a high percentage is chronically unemployed. Take away public sector jobs, the biggest source of employment in the county, and those at the handful of lumber operations, and there would be, well, not much left. Dirt and unimproved gravel roads throughout the county are dotted with sad houses without electricity and occupied by people living in bone-crushing poverty.

The landscape is naturally beautiful, dominated by hilly forest lands, including the Colville National Forest, and farms. It has produced a fiercely independent people, almost libertarian in bent with its mix of conservative rural values and alternative lifestyle seekers. The county once elected a commissioner who bragged about his membership in the John Birch Society, and then proceeded to dump him in the next election. A long-tenured judge was kicked out because he refused to allow a "constitutionalist", who didn't recognize the legitimacy of U.S. currency, to pay his property taxes in gold.

In this mix of strange politics and rugged natural beauty, Jess and Sacco had discovered Loon Lake but not before an exhaustive yet pleasurable exploration of all the lakes in the area. For various reasons, none of the other lakes they visited suited them. Some were too small to ski on. Others, such as the beautiful Coeur D'Alene Lake in nearby Idaho, made them feel as though they were on a huge sea and not a lake. But Loon Lake was a happy compromise of all they wanted, made even more so by the availability of the oversized lot on the north end.

The water was warm in the summer and ideally suited for swimming close to shore. Winters occasionally brought ice thick enough to skate on. Fish life was varied from kokanee to mackinaw to carp to the little sun fish the children loved to catch off the docks and keep in their buckets until they were dead. Ducks, herons and migrating geese were everywhere, as well as falcon life. And the local pride and joy was the resurgent loon population.

At 1,200 acres and measuring three miles in length with a varying width, the lake was large enough to ski on and not feel claustrophobic except on hot weekends in the summer when the crowd from Spokane, 35 miles to the south, headed out for relief. Jess thought the lake struck the perfect balance between familiarity and anonymity. He knew a pleasant number of people on the lake, at least well enough to talk to them over coffee. Many people knew him as well although it was only in passing.

The lake was named in 1881 by one of the early pioneers in the Colville Valley, John Hofstetter. Jess thought it would be interesting to know what the lake was known as before the white man arrived. The local library couldn't help and neither could the nearby tribal office for the Spokane Indians. "How sad," he thought, "that the language and culture of the local Indians have been so decimated that a landmark as significant as the lake has lost its identity."

Jess turned off the engine when he reached Ben's designated hole and readied his fishing gear. After dropping anchor and pulling out the line, he settled in for the most pleasant part of fishing – the gentle rocking of the boat and the drifting of the mind that accompanied it. During these times he thought about everything and nothing at the same time. Occasionally, he would bring a book to read but he was becoming increasingly comfortable just being alone with his own thoughts. At first, the pain had been a too-frequent invader of these moments. It was true, however, what they said about time healing.

All the elements conspired to make this a flawless outing. The temperature was a companionable 80 degrees. The sun was far along its descent with a slight glow of pink around the sparse clouds that surrounded it. There was an absolute minimum of intrusion from other boats on the water and there were no skiers or obnoxious jet skis.

The late afternoon had a docile feeling and he rocked peacefully back and forth in the boat with the tiny waves. He let his eyes transfix on the line and then on the water to which the line led. He heard nothing except the sporadic lapping of the water on the side of the boat, the intermittent sound of a distant loon, an almost plaintive tone, and, if he strained, the downshifting of trucks as they took the grade on the nearby highway into Spokane. He never nodded off during these otherwise restful times and he sometimes wondered why; nothing could be more relaxing. "It's like a form of divine meditation," he thought.

Jess shifted his weight and slid his pole along the side of the boat while he superstitiously caressed the handle of his rod. He whispered coaxingly to the unseen prey. He gazed. He breathed deeply and gazed again. He let time pass. There was a minute tug of his pole and he mentally debated whether it was more than wave action. He breathed deeply again and concentrated on expanding and contracting his chest as he inhaled and exhaled.

There was a soft thud on the side of the boat that was duller than the slap of a wave against the fiber glass. He slowly leaned forward and casually glanced into the water, not looking for anything in particular and not prepared for what he saw.

The burning started in his stomach and moved quickly upward to his throat. His face turned ashen and the heat from his skin disappeared until it was cold to the touch. The only sound he heard was the faint buzzing of an insect around his ear.

Jess knew this feeling. He thought, he prayed, he would never be visited by it again, but he was wrong. Before, it had kept him awake at nights restlessly tossing from side to side. But now he couldn't move. His muscles weren't getting the message his brain was desperately trying to send. Over and over he tried. His mind was screaming; his body was immobilized. Finally, he sprang forward over the side of the boat, almost losing his balance in the process.

He reached down, grabbing the slightly submerged body by the knap of its neck and lifted, enough to see its face. He didn't have to, however. He already knew who it was.

CHAPTER THREE

Just as the EMT's were lifting Gary Lother's body into the ambulance, Jess heard The Wail of a loon. In the darkness, the sound was amplified and seemed closer than it probably was. But it was loud nonetheless and clear – somewhere a loon was looking to be relieved of nest-bound egg warming responsibilities. In all likelihood, the nest would contain two of the mossy green and dark brown flecked eggs. At least that is what Gary Lother had taught Jess earlier in the summer. That and a lot more.

Jess vividly remembered meeting the stringy young fifteen-year old for the first time. It was late spring, long after the snow had melted and the foundation for the house had been poured and the walls and roof framed in. Jess took a rare break from the work of building the house to capture the day, a bright, sunny day that seemed to have the effect of polishing the green in all plant life. He rode his quiet Suzuki motorcycle, street legal but built for climbing impossible hills, to the top of Deer Lake Mountain, just a couple of miles to the northeast of the lake. From its summit of more than 3,700 feet, he had a 360 degree view for miles, a view which included Loon Lake to the southwest and Deer Lake to the northeast. It was the only place he knew of, short of an airplane, where you could see both lakes simultaneously. But to get there, he was required to ignore several "no trespassing" signs and to bypass a locked gate. He enjoyed the tiny thrill of harmless wrongdoing almost as much as the panoramic reward. "Besides," he rationalized, "if they **really** didn't want anyone up here, they would build these gates so you couldn't get past them so easily."

At the top, he warily circled the huge microwave tower, never sure of what carcinogenic affect proximity might have. Cellular phone transmission came at a price. On the side facing Loon Lake, he spotted the boy sitting down with his back against a tree, helmet on the ground beside him, and older dirt bike nearby.

"Hi," Jess offered, as he dismounted and turned the bike off. He noticed the wind was much stronger at this altitude than down below. "Want some water?" he asked, handing the canteen toward the boy. Off road bikers tend to be especially friendly toward one another, sharing as they do, a unique love of sport and the common adversity of those who criticize their sometimes intrusive presence in the woods.

"No, thank you," the boy said, barely looking up at Jess, appearing a little nervous or guilty. Jess wondered if the boy thought he was there to hassle him about trespassing. Jess sat down against a nearby tree and made himself comfortable.

"I like it up here. I like the view and I like the feeling it gives me to be able to see so far. How about you?"

The boy finally looked at Jess. "I like it, too," he said quietly.

"My name's Jess. Jess Stevens." He extended his hand which the boy took and shook somewhat unnaturally.

"I'm Gary Lother."

"You live around here, Gary?"

"Uh huh. Just off Loon Lake. We just moved there last winter."

"We just moved there, too. We're building a house there now. Let me show you." Jess broke out his expensive Bushnell binoculars from his day sack and handed them to Gary who didn't refuse the offer this time.

"Twelve by fifties? Wow! Pretty powerful."

"There. You see?" Jess said, pointing. "Right there on the north side of the lake. If you look closely, you can see the new lumber."

"Yeah, I can. That's your place, huh? I wondered whose that was. That's a big house."

"Well, it will be when it's done. Probably bigger than we need."

Gary stood up and continued to use the binoculars eagerly looking in all directions. Jess watched the skinny teenager with long brown hair and the complexion problems of a typical teenager. He struck Jess as a little sad or lonely.

"You get out on your bike very often?" Jess asked.

"Quite a bit. After school anyway. And on weekends when my Dad lets me." He said it without bitterness but as though the privilege was parsimoniously granted.

"Do you have any binoculars?"

"No, sir. Well, I do but not like these. Mine are seven by thirty-five's and, uh, one of the lenses is cracked."

"Tell you what. Why don't you borrow those for a couple of days and see what you can see from some of these other hilltops?" Jess swept his arm around at no peak in particular. "You can bring them back to me later. You know where I live."

Gary glanced down at the binoculars and back at Jess with a look of confusion on his face.

"I don't think I should," he said. His tone said he wanted to.

"Nonsense," Jess said with finality. "Do it. And maybe in return you can show me some good places to bike around here. Deal?" He stuck his hand out.

Gary took it. "Deal."

Thus began their tentative friendship. Gary, unsure of himself in general and especially around an adult, and Jess, not yet ready to let anybody in close except Sacco. The boy wasn't intimidated by Jess' importance – he wasn't even aware of Jess' past, which suited Jess just fine – but he was shy and sensitive. And he was self-sufficient, which Jess delighted in discovering when he hired him to help with some of the smaller chores during the final weeks of construction of the house. The boy was obviously intelligent and highly curious. Jess had had dozens of students like the boy over the years and they invariably excelled later in life.

Jess eventually learned the boy's father, Willie, was out of work on an industrial insurance claim. He was stern and almost angry about something. He took it out on Gary and his younger sister, Gloria, by yelling at them for just about anything. Once, when Jess and the boy returned home from motorcycling five minutes late, Willie met them in the yard and shouted obscenities at Gary, loud enough for the entire neighborhood to hear. Jess was tempted to intervene but kept his temper and his own counsel. Arguing with a drunk, which Willie often was, never got anyone anywhere.

It wasn't until one day early in the summer, when Jess took Gary out for a canoe ride on the lake, that he discovered how truly extraordinary the boy was.

They paddled – at first awkwardly but with progressive synchronization – over by the rush weeds and cattails and near one of the loon nests. This one had a floating sign nearby that read: "Quiet! Loon nest." It was one of many just like it around the lake that Gary had labored to construct and then secretly place in the water, hoping they would help protect the loons from well-meaning human activity.

"Do you know much about loons, Mr. Stevens?" he asked respectfully.

"Gary, if you don't start calling me Jess, I'm going to start calling you Mr. Lother." And you wouldn't want to be confused for your father he thought to himself.

"Yes, sir. Anyway, loons are the oldest birds in North America. They have fossil records dating back sixty million years. Sixty million years! And they mate for life. What's that word for that?"

"Unusual," Jess teased. "No, actually, it's monogamous."

As they meandered through the rushes, the boy whispered in an almost prayerful tone about the loon. About the bird's lack of grace on land and speed in the air. About the loon's unique diving abilities — up to 200 feet below water's surface. And about the bird's migration patterns.

The two also fished and water skied together and rode their bikes as often as Jess would allow himself a break from construction. Over time, they spent hours and hours in the hills around Loon Lake among the Douglas firs and Ponderosa pines. They relished trespassing on Boise Cascade forest property despite the most foreboding of gates and fences. It was a shared guilty pleasure.

Once, Jess took the boy sky diving at the Spokane Jump Center. They jumped tandem, hooked to one another, from 12,000 feet. Jess ordinarily took first-timers out at less than 9,000 feet but the higher altitude allowed for a video tape to be made which Jess wanted the boy to have. From 12,000 feet, the free fall lasted more than a minute and enabled the camera person to jump and get set up for some of the minute-plus free fall. Except for talking about the loons, the boy usually didn't say much to Jess or vice versa but after the jump, Gary was downright animated in his enthusiasm. It was the one time Jess thought the boy didn't seem slightly sad or tragic.

Jess was concerned about approaching Mr. Lother before the jump. Although Jess had more than 1,200 jumps in his log book, including 120 tandem jumps, he knew the idea struck most people as just this side of insane. But Lother surprised him.

"How much will this cost?" was all he asked. No mention was made of the boy's safety at all. "It's on the house," Jess answered and Lother just grunted assent and took another swig of his beer.

"Jess. Jess. Hey, Jess! Anybody home in there?" Finally, Jess was literally shaken from his trance by the firm grip of Stevens County Sheriff Bill Page. "Are you all right?"

"What? Huh? Oh, yeah. Sure. I'm, uh, fine, Bill."

"Is this your first time, Jess? With a body?" The questions were obviously asked out of concern.

The two men had met many years ago at a Stevens County Democratic Party picnic in Colville, less than an hour to the north on Highway 395. Jess loved to drop in on Stevens County political events and make jokes about his namesake county.

Stevens County was named for Washington's first territorial governor, Isaac Ingalls Stevens, a man appointed governor before he had ever laid eyes on the Northwest, thanks to an old classmate, President Franklin Pierce, in whose 1852 presidential campaign Stevens had helped. Governor Stevens was arrogant and heavy handed in his efforts to "settle" the "Indian question." He even went so far as to arrest a territorial Supreme Court Justice at gun point when the justice dared to disagree legally with him. In 1854 Stevens signed into law the legislation organizing and naming the counties in eastern Washington including one named for himself. In 1857 he left for the "other Washington" to serve as a territorial representative to Congress. He eventually served as a union general in the Civil War and was killed in 1862 leading a charge at Chantilly, Virginia, thus becoming Washington State's most distinguished Civil War hero. Jess pondered the irony that it might have been one of his confederate ancestors who actually killed the erstwhile Governor.

Jess and Sheriff Page had become casual friends through contact in the summer and working together occasionally in Olympia, the state capital. Jess respected the Sheriff a great deal for his professionalism and because he never imposed upon Jess' friendship. But they didn't know one another well enough for the Sheriff to have known he didn't need to ask the question about Jess being around a body. Like a lot of people their age, they didn't talk much about it.

"No, Bill. It isn't," was all Jess said. He didn't say anymore and Page intuitively grasped the implication.

"Where were you?"

"I Corps." It was a military designation for the northernmost region of South Vietnam during the war. It was also the area where the bloodiest conflicts occurred.

"Which branch? What year?" the Sheriff asked.

"Marines. 1968."

The Sheriff asked no further questions. He knew what being a Marine in I Corps meant in 1968.

Jess didn't talk about his experiences in Vietnam at all. He refused to trade upon them even when it might have done him some good and been perfectly appropriate, or at least, acceptable. He probably said more to Bill Page just then about his service than he had in the previous ten years. Not once did he mention it during his courtship with Sacco. Somehow, she knew he had been to Vietnam but she never asked him about it or about the scar on his right shoulder. She only accidentally discovered his decorations, including the Purple Heart, that were now stored in the bottom of Sacco's cedar wedding chest.

"I was a medical corpsman assigned to the Marines out of Da Nang about the same time." Page let it drop and would never bring it up again. "Did you know the boy?"

"What? Oh, Gary? Yeah, I knew him." Jess' mind was somewhere else. "He was helping me on the house. And I . . . I just bought him a pair of good binoculars. I never had the chance to give them to him."

The Sheriff put his hand on Jess' shoulder. It was a gesture of kindness and concern. "I'm sorry, Jess. It's awful tough with the young ones."

Jess looked at him but said nothing, grateful for the gesture. He thought it unusually warm for the Sheriff, who was usually all business and professional. At six foot one and with a straight back, trim body and closely cropped hair, he looked more the part of a FBI agent than a small county sheriff. But he was damn good at his job. Even though he claimed not to understand the politics associated with running for elective office, the truth was obviously quite different. He ran and won in his first effort eleven years before when the people of Stevens County, despite a streak of arch conservative independence, were more than ready to move beyond the frontier fisticuffs approach the previous sheriff had employed. On the strength of his professionalism and performance, he had been uncontested ever since.

Page never thought he would be an elected sheriff but he served twelve years in the Washington State Patrol and finally tired of the frequent transfers required to be promoted. In any event, the job agreed with him; although in his late forties, he looked more like he was still in his thirties.

"You know, Jess, these drownings bother me as much as anything I have to deal with. They always seem so senseless and avoidable. I bet I have had ten of them since I first got into office. Last year, I had one over at Deer Lake. A skiing accident. Two years ago I had one up at Jump Off Joe Lake. A boy out alone in a canoe who didn't know how to swim and didn't have a life jacket on. It's frustrating. The department has put a lot of effort into teaching water safety in the schools and in patrolling the lakes. But we just don't seem to be able to instill the common sense necessary to avoid this."

The two men watched as the ambulance doors were closed and the attendant turned to the Sheriff for instructions.

"Sorry, Jess. I guess I just don't look forward to talking to the boy's parents. That part of this job doesn't ever get easier. In fact, I think it gets harder all the time."

"Bill, I'm not sure the boy drowned." Their eyes met and the Sheriff held the look while he digested the weight of Jess' words.

Their silence was pierced by the eerie, almost human laugh sound emitted by the loon and known as The Tremolo. It was an alarm call.

CHAPTER FOUR

J ess Stevens believed – no, he
knew – there were few songs
more beautiful or inspirational than *Amazing Grace*. It
didn't matter whether one was particularly religious or
not, the song transcended theology. And the nature of
its origin, written by a repentant slave trader as he listened to the mournful chorus of his human cargo during
his last Atlantic crossing, made it even more so. The powerful rendition being offered at Gary Lother's memorial
service confirmed Jess' affection for the song.

The singer didn't know the Lother boy or his family
and she wasn't even a member of the small United Church
of Christ congregation whose number expanded and con-
tracted with the summer season at Loon Lake. Instead,
she was one of the artists-in-residence in the area who
volunteered her talent for the service. Someone said she
had lost a favorite nephew to drowning. Now in her early
sixties, she was once a noteworthy regional opera per-
former. It didn't sound to Jess like she had lost any of her
musical prowess.

The small, traditional white chapel stood in the middle
of the tiny town of Loon Lake, kitty corner from the Loon
Lake grade school and just a mile from the Stevens' house.
Today it was hot to the point of being stifling, made more

so by the standing room only crowd and the hard, wooden pews with people seated shoulder to shoulder.

"Interesting crowd, don't you think?" Sacco whispered to him. Jess managed a nod. "The Lothers haven't lived here that long and they sure haven't been active in the community but look at the people," she continued. Again, he just nodded. "I always thought people here liked the isolation that living on the lake gave them, liked being left alone. I guess it takes a tragedy to bring them together even for newcomers like the Lothers."

Nearly every student from the high school was present, the same youngsters who, a week before, wouldn't have much to do with Gary, the loner and relative new-comer. The boys sat in stunned and confused silence. Most of the girls were crying, a few uncontrollably. Willie Lother and his wife, Juanita, sat in the front pew with their sole remaining child, Gloria, a beautiful blonde eight year-old. Emotionally, Gloria didn't have a clue as to what this was all about. She had no frame of reference to help understand permanent loss; the concept was completely foreign to her. If she had been asked about it, she would have responded with a question, "You mean Gary is **never** coming back?" And so, Gloria sat passively and politely attentive, aware on some level that serious behavior on her part was the only acceptable course.

"God's love for His children is special. Jesus taught us about this love in the nineteenth book of Matthew, verses thirteen and fourteen. 'Then children were brought to him that he might lay his hands on them and pray. The disciples rebuked the people; but Jesus said, Let the children come to me, and do not hinder them; for to such belongs the kingdom of heaven.' "

The young minister droned on with routine and pre-dictable scripture passages. This church was his first as-signment and he strained and struggled with every new task to make a good impression and to be helpful. It had not consciously occurred to him that this was his first funeral service for a child. He was charged with spiritual faith but young. Only the faith that comes from experience would prepare him to ease the pain of a life taken before its fullness.

Jess sat holding Sacco's hand the entire service. He never looked up and barely moved except to wipe the beading sweat from his forehead. He didn't join in either prayer or song. Few people in the church knew what self-discipline his presence was requiring. Sacco knew.

"You okay?" she asked two different times. He just nodded and squeezed her hand. If he had looked up, he would have seen the tears dripping silently down her cheeks.

"Please join me in praying the prayer taught to us by the Lord. 'Our Father Who Art in Heaven . . .'" The minister finally concluded the service and mercifully dismissed the congregation to the cooler outside air.

People lingered. The stifling heat was too fresh in their minds to hop right in their cars and be oven baked immediately. With no internment ceremony ahead, they just milled around speaking in the hushed collective tones that are appropriately respectful of the dead while waiting their turn to extend condolences to the Lothers.

"Come on, Gumbah. Let's go say something to the Lothers," Sacco urged Jess but he didn't move.

"I know you don't want to but I also know you will regret it if you don't. And I know today has been hard on you. Just think what it has been like for Mr. and Mrs. Lother." Sacco knew what was on Jess' mind and she intuitively knew what to say and how to say it.

"Okay," he relented.

They moved toward the Lothers the first time the grieving parents appeared to be left alone for a moment.

Mrs. Lother was still struggling with her anguish and had a difficult time stopping her crying long enough to greet people and thank them for attending. Willie Lother was much more stoic although he seemed quite uncomfortable with the whole affair. It might have been the suit he was wearing which was at least one size too small. His shirt buttons were tight on his beer belly and the tie he wore was ten years out of style.

"Mr. Lother, my wife and I just wanted you to know we . . ." That was as far as Jess got before Lother unexpectedly exploded.

"What are you doing here Stevens?" he demanded. Jess was dumb struck.

"You've got some nerve being here, you son of a bitch. You think I'm so stupid I don't know who pulled the strings to get the autopsy done on my boy. Donchya'?" He was yelling now.

"Well, I'm not, you son of a bitch and I will never, **never,** forget that you had them cut my boy all up. I owe you one, ya' bastard!" With that, he cocked his arm and fist to hit Jess who stood staring Lother in the eye without moving. Sacco couldn't tell if he was still too stunned to react or if he was trying to stare Lother down. She swiftly stepped between the two men, which confused Lother, and then she grabbed Jess by the arm and pulled him in the direction of their car. Juanita Lother, by the time she realized what was going on at all, wailed even louder.

"What was all that about?" Sacco asked when they were out of earshot.

"Well, just what he said, paisan. I pulled a few strings and made sure the boy had an autopsy. It wasn't hard to do."

"Not on you but what about them?"

"It was the prudent thing to do," he answered.

"Is 'prudent' the same thing as the 'right thing'?"

Jess looked at her sideways as they walked and wished she were a little less pointed. He opened the driver's side of the car to let the hot air escape and leaned on the window without saying anything. "What would you have done if he had swung?" he asked, trying to change the subject.

"Well, I was prepared to duck. What would you have done?"

"I don't know," he said after a pause. She knew he was right and it frightened her.

"Well," she added trying to lighten the moment, "look on the bright side. At least he was sober. No telling how loud or violent he would have gotten if he had been drunk."

Just then, Sheriff Page walked up. "Hi, Jess. Hi, Sacco. I was hoping I would have a chance to see you here." The Sheriff was dressed in his formal uniform which he rarely wore but looked quite impressive in. "I talked to the medical examiner this morning about the autopsy report."

"This is timely, Bill," Jess responded with an irony lost on the Sheriff. "What did he say?"

"**She** said that there was no evidence of external injuries, no contusions, no abrasions or lacerations or anything around the head or neck or anywhere for that matter, to indicate trauma of any kind. Second, she said the toxicological work-up revealed no evidence of disease or drugs or other possible contributory causes."

"This isn't exactly enlightening yet, Bill."

"Wait. I'm not done. Evidently, Gary had eaten not too long before he died. His stomach was full but the gastric contents were barely aspirated."

"Aspirated? You mean full of water?"

"Basically, yes. And neither were his lungs. Barely aspirated that is."

"What the hell does that mean, Bill?"

"Well, it means the coroner ruled that Gary Lother died between nine PM and three AM the evening of August 23rd of accidental drowning."

Jess furrowed his brow and squinted his eyes ever so slightly in the manner of someone who is confused. "I don't understand, Bill. I thought you just said he didn't have any water in the lungs. How can that be?"

"Water isn't always found in the lungs of drown victims although it almost always is. In fact, death by drowning is a diagnosis by exclusion. In effect, the medical examiner rules everything out and then makes a determination on the basis of what's left and the context. The boy was found floating in the water with no external injuries and no evidence of drugs."

"Listen to me, Bill." Jess' voice and body almost visibly coiled into a steel-hard determination. "Gary Lother did not drown! I've been water skiing with that young man many times. He was a regionally competitive swimmer at school. He was the best swimmer on this lake. Furthermore, he possessed more common sense than any student I have ever known. And I'm telling you: Gary Lother did not drown!" The last words were as much spit out as they were spoken.

The Sheriff let the words hang in the air as he absorbed the strength of Jess' conviction. Finally, with quiet reason and empathy and without condescension he asked, "If it wasn't drowning, Jess, what was it?"

CHAPTER FIVE

J ess was trying hard not to show the irritation of having his new home and sanctuary invaded by large numbers of increasingly rowdy people. After all, it was to have been his refuge. And it was a beautiful one at that. He even managed a little pride in his work as he gazed over the large A-frame house with the expensive cedar siding from his vantage point on the second floor deck outside his bedroom. "At least up here it is a little quiet," he thought.

He was satisfied with the quality of workmanship all the way from top to bottom. He didn't even mind the dowdy looks of the steep aluminum roof. "There is beauty in practicality," he mused as he considered the benefits of the metal roof in the middle of winter with the sometimes punishing snows of the area. Jess had one small regret, however. The wood stove in the corner of his bedroom was a waste and he wished he had not put it in. He thoroughly enjoyed cutting wood and he loved the romance of the wood fire. But he hated the thought of contributing to an already dirty airscape. It was a well kept secret that the Spokane area to the south had the second most polluted metropolitan air shed in the United States, second only to Los Angeles. The conservative people of Spokane violently disagreed with the air sampling methodology every time they were reminded of their standing. Maybe he could convert the stove to natural gas later.

He was particularly proud of the special touches he had added to the house such as the electronic dumbwaiter in the upstairs bedroom that went all the way to the utility room in the basement. It spared Sacco and him from constantly running up and down two flights, a form of exercise he found only slightly more tedious than jogging. The computer system was state of the art and fed to all parts of the house and onto the beach through an elaborate control system in a main floor panel. Every convenience imaginable was present, from special recycling bins to an extra large and heavy duty trash compactor to a driveway wired to melt the heavy winter snows without shoveling. Jess installed a powerful central vacuum system and two over-sized hot water heaters to accommodate his long morning showers with Sacco. Money had been no object, and so he spent it.

Today, the entire house, except for the second floor, was being socially inaugurated with the start-of-the-school-year party for Sacco's staff and their spouses. It was this intrusion that put Jess on edge. He didn't like the crowd. He didn't like them walking in and out of his home, through every room in the house, gawking at the expense of the furnishings. He resented their loudness and he was damn sure someone was taking bathroom liberties in the hot tub two floors below on the patio. Right now, the hot tub, built for four, was occupied by five people all of whom had had too much wine or beer. Teachers were rarely hard alcohol drunks. It probably had to do with their relatively low wages.

"Penny?"

"Oh, hi paisan." Jess spoke absently to Sacco as she approached him. "Just enjoying the view."

"Horse shit," she said evenly and without anger. She

never said bull shit, always horse shit, and Jess often wondered where she got the expression since she rarely swore at all.

"You're still stewing about the Lother boy. I recognize that mood in you. And besides, you haven't been sleeping well. Did you know that?"

"Yeah, I suppose you're right." He was still looking down when he answered.

"Look, Gumbah. You're angst ain't getting you anywhere and if you don't give yourself a swift kick where it is needed soon, I will." He couldn't tell if she was being serious or not. She wasn't smiling and didn't appear especially angry. He turned toward her to be able to better read her. "Furthermore, I am making do the best I can with my new job and responsibilities. If you are going to stay up here and mope all afternoon, well, frankly, I think I would prefer you went golfing or motorcycling. I have to work with these people – I am supposed to lead them – and I am not particularly interested in them leaving here thinking I am married to an asshole even if you are one sometimes."

Now there was no doubt in his mind as to her seriousness. As always, it worked.

"Touché', darling. I will go do what I do best: grip and grin, meet and greet."

He kept his promise, wandering through the house making himself as available and charming as only Jess Stevens could. He gave tours of his home, clearly the most beautiful in the region. He took people out on the Bayliner for quick spins around the lake. He quickly, humorously and modestly extricated himself from the overly flirtatious advances of not one, but two, inebriated women. He regaled small groups with great stories about his days in the classroom. And he listened with great interest – and some longing – as several described the events of this year's beginning. He admitted to himself that he missed teaching but not enough to return any more than he contemplated returning to his other passion.

"Mr. Speaker." Jess froze. Barney Rubble stuck out his hand. "How are you?"

For the first time in over an hour, Jess was uncomfortable again. Nonetheless, he collected the large paw of the high school's science and vocational agriculture teacher, George "Barney" Rubble, whose life or at least name, was changed by a television cartoon. Rubble was an excellent teacher. His Future Farmers of America (FFA) program had rescued many a student from ruin. He worked tirelessly after school to provide some meaningful activities for students who would otherwise find substantially less constructive ways to spend their time. It always surprised people that he had such rapport with students. He was an older teacher, in his late fifties, personally conservative with the out of date crew cut to prove it, and without a whole lot of personality.

"Hi, Barney," Jess finally managed. He had not been called Mr. Speaker in several months. It was a title he was never particularly comfortable with even during his near-record tenure in that lofty position in the Washington State House of Representatives. Jess lacked pretense and it endeared him to his colleagues, the press and his constituents.

But it was his integrity that made Jess stand out and catapulted him to Speaker, somewhat reluctantly, on the heels of a scandal involving his predecessor. His word was gold in an environment where the shelf life of a promise often extended no further than the next conversation. His internal compass always pointed to doing the right thing and he wasn't pious or sanctimonious about it. In fact, he didn't even talk about it in those terms. It was simply implicit in his actions.

He cared a great deal about the institution in which he served. He loved (and taught) its history and could cite it at strategic times. He often asked his colleagues and his staff questions like, "How is this action or policy going to hold up over time and how will it reflect on the House?" Because of this he was trusted and respected.

Jess also cared about the people he represented in a personal way. He never burned with the ambition to run for the legislature until he read a story in the newspaper about a woman who lost her entire arm in a climbing accident. The only place she could get an upper arm prosthesis and be trained in its use was at a state facility that denied her assistance because it served industrial accident victims exclusively. Jess thought that was plain cruel and he vowed to do something about it. In his first term, he did.

Barney Rubble's reference to Jess' former title broke the code. Several teachers slowly began to migrate toward Jess and Barney. No one wanted to bring up the subject of Jess Stevens, the powerful but abruptly retired Speaker of the House, for fear of whatever unintended consequence it might bring. And while few fully understood the significance of what Jess had been, they were all aware on some level that the Speaker was generally considered the second most powerful person in Washington's political system, next only to the governor.

Politics was an uneasy subject for Jess. People related to him differently when they talked about politics, as though he became the role and ceased being the person. Besides, one never knew when a seemingly harmless discussion would erupt into disagreement and anger. So Jess deflected their questions leading them back to discussion of the coming school year so skillfully they were unaware he was changing the subject.

Jess enjoyed listening to the conversation about schools and students. It was always fun to hear teachers dissect the nuances of young people's behavior. He often thought teachers were the original sociologists with their sensitivity and powers of observation on the subtleties of group behavior and organization.

"Hey, Jess. How about coming into class and doing some guest lecturing?" The request came from one of the younger teachers in Sacco's building, a history and social studies teacher. Jess had met him briefly earlier in the summer and taken a liking to him. He was still full of enthusiasm and ideas and had successfully published a simulation board game now in distribution throughout the country. The young man had all the ingredients of a successful teacher: he loved his subject matter, he loved the kids, and he loved the act of teaching. "Besides, the kids would benefit a lot from your experiences. To say nothing of us. How 'bout it?"

The teacher knew the request would be a difficult one for Jess but he made it anyway. Jess didn't know at the time but it was prearranged with Sacco. The conversations quickly grew quiet awaiting Jess' response.

"Sure. Why not?" Jess didn't really want to do any teaching right now and didn't want to be around large numbers of people, but all the talk about school and the students sparked a yearning for chalkboard dust that had never entirely left him, even in his most successful days in the legislature.

CHAPTER SIX

Jess vividly recalled the first time he went sky diving. "I suppose everybody does," he thought to himself. He went tandem – securely fastened to an instructor – with an old high school friend, Bill Van Buren. Bill owned a plane and kept it stored at a jump center where he spent most weekends taking people for the "I've-always-wanted-to-do-that" thrill of their lives. Jess was no exception. The first time he went, he shut down emotionally. From the moment the airplane left the runway, he felt absolutely nothing. In fact, he was much more scared his second time. Maybe because he knew a little of what to expect; or maybe because he knew enough to know better.

Today he was more enthusiastic than usual. Jumping had become anything but routine but still, some days were better than others. And today was better if for no other reason than it was beautiful.

He was jumping at 13,000 feet to take maximum advantage of the experience he often described as "better than sex." Many of his friends had ridiculed him for that expression but not those who had taken him up on his challenge to try it for themselves.

He popped the door open at just over 12,000 feet and then rechecked his equipment to make sure all was well. He could never forget the tragic but darkly humorous story of the veteran jumper who died because he literally forgot to put his pack on. Jess hoped jumping would never become that familiar to him.

He placed one hand on the wing support and eased his feet out onto the small platform below the door. Gazing over the countryside, he oriented himself by identifying the many lakes in the region. Even Couer d'Alene and Priest Lakes over the nearby border in Idaho were visible at this altitude.

When Jess was comfortable he threw his hands and arms back at a 45 degree angle to the wing while arching the small of his back as hard as he could, until it hurt. The first time he jumped he forgot to arch and the predictable result was that he fell face up and then when he tried to right himself, he rolled over and over.

He smiled as he fell, almost laughing at the thrill of it. He loved this, everything about it. The speed. The panorama. The loud roar of the cold air around him. Because of the sound and the thrill, he was convinced that sky diving was the true origin of the word "rush." Later, he would be equally delighted by the virtual silence a fully engaged chute would bring. Again, he remembered his first jumping experience which was a tandem jump. When the chute deployed, he was startled by the sudden silence and peace. It was so quiet, he spoke in whispers to Bill on his back.

"I'm alive!" he screamed with joy into the void of noisy space.

The one minute it took to get to 5,000 feet – where he would pull the rip chord to the chute – went altogether too fast although with experience, he learned to stretch the time through in-air acrobatics that varied his speed. To himself, he repeated the chutist's litany: "Arch. Look. Reach and pull." The rip cord came out of its slot as it had a thousand times before. He mentally braced for the familiar jolt of the chute's opening and the instant braking of his motion. Instead, there was nothing. He continued to free fall.

He looked at the rip cord and realized nothing had happened. Ordinarily, he would stuff the cord into his pack before reaching upward for the handles to guide the chute. This time he just tossed it into space and reached for the ancillary cord on the small of his back. This had never happened to him before but he wasn't panicked. The equipment was expensive and designed to avoid tragedies in situations like these.

It was slightly awkward to reach and pull the ancillary cord but he managed to do so before he had fallen much farther. The altimeter on his wrist read just below 4,000 feet, ample time for the chute to deploy. "Some military experts don't pull until 1,500 feet," he said to no one.

He thought how this was the first "incident" he had ever experienced while diving. And he thought how lucky he was to be in this situation rather than one Bill once encountered when he got caught up in the main chute opening and almost didn't get unraveled. Bill severely broke his leg while landing that time. Jess knew landing with the emergency chute would be rough, too, and he was beginning to prepare himself for the pain of impact. Only the emergency chute didn't open and Jess immediately realized he was going to die in a matter of seconds.

His first thought was to give brief thanks that Sacco had not come to watch today. At least she would be spared the horror of his hideous ending. Jess had read what would happen to his body; it would literally explode like a water balloon – which it was – and his body parts would be scattered yards away. The impact would create a several inch cavity in the ground no matter how hard it was, even if it was full of rocks.

"I love you, Sacco," he said to her, hoping and thinking that she would somehow know she was his last thought, that she would somehow feel his affection one last time. He was stabbed by regret as the images of them running, sitting in the hot tub and making love flashed through his mind. He saw her lying next to him on their bed, naked and un-covered, raised up on one elbow with an impish grin on her face indicating her pleasure with his performance.

Panic seeped into his stomach as the ground moved closer and closer. Only seconds remaining. The altimeter read 2,000 feet. His mind made one last futile review of the check list of actions in emergencies. No contingencies left. No chance. At least he wouldn't feel anything.

Jess could now discern the people on the ground and there was something about them, even though he could not see their faces or their expressions, that told him they knew. And then he was overwhelmed by the terror of it all. The ground was very close and closing in on him as though it would swallow him. It was the last few hundred feet and then it was almost upon him. And he screamed one last scream of terror before he hit.

"Jess! Jess!" Sacco had panic in her voice as she rushed to the floor beside the bed. Jess hit his head hard when he fell and it rapidly brought him out of his fitful sleep.

He wore nothing and although it was a cool evening his body was drenched with sweat. He curled his knees up to his chest and wrapped his arms around them. "Oh, no," he wailed. "Please, not again, God. Please." He sobbed out loud.

Sacco sat next to him, also naked, and wrapped her arms tightly around him and gently rocked him. "Shhh. Shhh, Gumbah. It's all right. I'm here. I'm here," she whispered.

After a few minutes, when the sobbing subsided, she reached up and pulled the comforter down and covered their bodies with it and continued to rock him and kiss him gently on the cheek and neck.

When his shivers stopped, Jess rose and walked silently out onto the deck and stood at the railing, arm in arm with Sacco. After half an hour of staring at the reflection of the moon on the lake's surface he spoke without turning his head. "I cannot go through this again, Sacco. Being on the lake isn't enough; it isn't protection. I only have one choice."

"I know, Jess." Her use of his given name signaled her true understanding of his feelings. "I don't know how you are going to do it or even if you are. But I know how important it is to you."

He didn't know how he was going to do it either but Jess knew he would prove that Gary Lother had been murdered.

CHAPTER SEVEN

Not far from the Stevens' lake place was an idyllic farm nestled along the Jump Off Joe Road that ran from the Springdale highway north to Jump Off Joe Lake. The farm was three hundred acres of timber, hay, and a few cattle, depending on prices. It was owned and operated by two brothers fifteen years apart in age. It was called "Hidden Valley" although no sign marked its neat entrance.

Hidden Valley had been in the family for nearly a hundred years and was left to the brothers when their parents died in a grisly head-on collision with a drunk driver on State Highway 395 out of Colville. Naturally, the offending driver walked away unscathed and practically unbruised so anesthetized was his nervous system. He walked away legally, too. It was prior to Mothers Against Drunk Driving, an organized form of protest against promiscuous highway slaughter.

There was a sister in the family as well. Her name was Edwina but people called her Edie. She was the oldest, nearly 23 at the time of the accident. Edie assumed parenting responsibilities for her brothers, especially the younger one who was only seven. The middle child, the older brother, was finishing college at Washington State University in Pullman at the time of the accident.

Edie was homely with big features, wide set eyes and a face that did not know how to smile. Her shoulders sagged with an unnamed grief even before her parents' death. People in the area felt sorry for her and whispered how sad it was she had no life of her own. They were shocked and slightly indignant two years later, however, when she announced she would be marrying a soldier from the Fairchild Air Force Base near Spokane and moving to town. They did not approve of the older brother assuming the parenting role for the younger boy. After all, he couldn't serve as a substitute mother and he hadn't even been out of school that long and besides, he had both a job and the farm to keep up.

On her wedding day, Edie managed something short of pretty but considerably more pleasing than usual. The entire community turned out to wish her well, momentarily forgetting her desertion of the youngest sibling. She had a very traditional wedding from white flowing dress to music to flower girl and ring bearer. Walking down the shiny hardwood aisle in Chewelah's United Methodist Church, she slipped on a flower petal. People later speculated that it was because she was wearing high heels which nobody could recall seeing her wear before that day.

When she fell, she hit her head on the floor and died instantly. The accident was so bizarre that it was written up in *Life* magazine. The community completely forgot her prospective indiscretion.

"Tommy," she said to her younger brother at the back of the church before the ceremony began, "It will be all right. We will come and visit you almost every weekend and you can come and stay with us, too. On holidays and in the summer. And we can go out to the base and walk around and look at the planes and go into downtown Spokane to movies. You'd like that, wouldn't you?"

Tommy was not consoled. He stood rigidly staring at the ground and at his highly polished shoes, fidgeting with the rented tuxedo that served as a uniform for his role as ring bearer. Finally, long after the ceremony was scheduled to begin, she gave up on her efforts and signaled for the processional to start. Two minutes later she was dead. Tommy was the first person to her side after the fall. Life had already left her eyes. He rose and left the church without saying another word and walked the ten miles back to the farm.

The farm had a small family cemetery on it. Tommy's parents and twenty-two relatives from over the last century were buried there, mostly small children or infants. That is where he went when he arrived home from the wedding that was not to be. He stood expressionless at his parents' grave sites for four hours before his older brother would discover where he was. It would be his last visit to the family cemetery. He even refused to attend the burial of his sister a few days later.

*   *   *

Early the same morning Jess had fallen out of bed with his nightmare, Tommy stood in the middle of the large open area just outside their modest but immaculate three bedroom home. He anxiously awaited the departure of Big Brother and the solitude it would bring. He had on his customary dress – combat boots and an Army jacket from his bygone days, well worn blue jeans and a colored tee shirt. Later in the day, as the temperature rose, the jacket would be shed and maybe even his shirt.

From a distance he looked younger than his middle-aged years. At five foot eight and 140 pounds, he was downright thin and lacked any of the paunch usually associated with middle age. His fine features, blue eyes and long, light brown hair, mostly unkempt, added to the age deception. Up close, however, the illusion dissolved. He wasn't sinewy so much as he was nearly anorexic. His eyes were heavily lined and nervous. And his skin was surprisingly light, almost pallid, for one who supposedly worked outside for a living.

Big Brother crawled into the pickup that was as clean and orderly as everything on the farm. It looked as though it had been driven off the showroom floor the day before even though it was six years old.

He rolled the window down and stuck his head out, craning his neck in the process. "Stay at it, little brother. There is plenty of work to do around here."

The younger brother waved him off in a neutral fashion. His feelings weren't neutral, however. He was tired, real tired, of Big Brother's supervisory ways. Big Brother told him what to do every single morning of every single day. He made daily lists of chores and then checked them at night against Tommy's progress. Sometimes it made Tommy sorry he had moved back to the farm. After all, he was an adult, too. He didn't need this smothering guidance of Big Brother.

He walked back up the driveway and through the back door to the kitchen. He wanted his morning shot of coffee before the full day began even though he had been up a couple of hours already. That was another thing: Big Brother always woke up so early, too early, and made him get up too.

Tommy opened a kitchen cabinet and took down the good china cup and saucer, keepsakes of his parents, that he liked to use and then wash out and put away before Big Brother arrived home after his day at his regular job. He poured the coffee and let it cool slightly while he retrieved the Coffeemate from another cupboard. Big Brother hated Coffeemate and it was a good thing.

He sat down and looked out the window toward the valley and the road. He opened the jar and laughed at the joke. "Coffeemate," he giggled out loud. With a spoon he dipped in ever so slightly until he had less than a gram of the white powder. He stirred it into his coffee and then momentarily relished the pleasure before his first sip. It would not take very long for the methamphetamine to affect him. As it did nearly every morning.

CHAPTER EIGHT

"Are you sure?" she asked. They sat naked in the hot tub soaking up the heat of the water and enjoying the view.

"Well, yeah. Sure I'm sure," he answered tentatively.

"You know the risk?"

"Of course, I know the risk. It's illegal, pure and simple."

"Have you thought about the effect this could have on others?" she asked him evenly.

"Yes, I think so. If you mean you, well, I'm not sure. I think, I'm just not sure but I think, well, it would be me and not you . . . and I'm not sure." His voice trailed off as he spoke in an uncharacteristically halting manner.

"Have you considered hiring this done? You don't have to do this yourself. In fact, you really don't know how. And you could pay someone to do it. It's not as though we can't afford it."

This was the first time Sacco had ever referred to their new-found wealth. Except for taking some of their small fortune to build and furnish their place at the lake and buy the boat, none of the money had been spent and it had never been talked about. It wasn't so much a source of embarrassment as of pain. Consequently, they entered into an implicit pact of silence about it.

She let it hang in the air for a minute until she sensed he wasn't going to answer.

"Are you sure they're not home? Absolutely sure? Sure, like **my** life depended on it?"

"Yes. Absolutely. Ben told me yesterday over at Granite Point. Willie Lother had been in the day before and told him they were taking off for a week to see Juanita's folks because he thought that might calm her down. Evidently, he isn't any better at that than he is anything else." Jess never did like the man and Lother's treatment of him at the boy's funeral was still fresh in his mind.

"That's a little cruel, don't you think, Gumbah?" He didn't answer. "I don't care for the man either but I think it's obvious he's angry with you and everybody else because on some level, he hasn't lived up to his own expectations at all. Think about what a burden it would be to go through every day considering yourself a failure. To your wife, to your kids and yourself."

"Fine, paisan. Go ahead and be compassionate. Give him the name of a psychologist or two. I just happen to think the man is a prick."

They stared one another down for several seconds until he relented in mock anger: "Look, if you're going to reproach me all the time, at least have the decency not to be right **all** the time." Satisfied he had finally understood, she said nothing.

They paused a while to savor the night sky and the stars. Unlike their previous home near Puget Sound on the other side of the state, here the night sky was vivid and bursting with stars as is only possible when far removed from the bleaching lights of a city.

Jess tipped his glass of ginger ale to her and said, "Give me my Sacco and take her and cut her out in little stars and she will make the face of heaven so fine that all the world will fall in love with night and pay no heed to the garish sun."

"Do you have any idea what you're looking for?"

"Well, a little affection is what I was leading up to."

"No, not that. I mean at the house."

"Oh, that. Sure. A clue, of course. Does this mean you don't find my liberties with The Bard to be romantic?"

"What would constitute a 'clue'?" she asked, ignoring his question.

"Well, now that you mention it, I don't know. I thought I'd just play it by ear."

"If you are open to suggestions . . . I would be looking for anything that is out of place, anything that doesn't seem to fit. And if you are bound and determined to proceed, get on with it. I don't want to be up all night waiting for Sheriff Page to call and ask if I can raise bail for you." It was her way of granting final permission if not blessing to her husband's questionable scheme.

Jess slowly moved over to the other side of the hot tub and kissed her on the lips before lifting himself out. He entered the house and quickly climbed the stairs to the bedroom where he dressed for the occasion. He put on blue jeans, a dark tee shirt and grabbed a pair of leather dress gloves with a thin wool lining. "A small fingerprint antidote," he thought.

The hardest decision was what pair of shoes to wear. Finally, he decided on a pair of old, dark, slip-on Rockports. Quiet and comfortable. And with a reasonably worn sole that could not be easily detected later. But despite these precautions, he was vaguely familiar enough with modern forensics to know that if the sheriff's office wanted to know who had been in the Lother house, they would find him.

In the garage, he brought out his Klein bike. Some of the mile or so distance to the Lother's could be covered, if necessary, through the woods on paths so familiar to him the darkness would be no impediment. He liked the combined flexibility and speed his bike gave him.

As he rode through the moonless night, Jess reasoned that there were four challenges ahead. First, to gain entry to the Lother home. That shouldn't be a problem since he had once seen Gary retrieve a hidden key from under the porch. Assuming it was still there.

Second, would be the boy's room. Jess wondered if it would still have the boy's possessions or if Juanita had packed everything up and sold it or given it away or done with it whatever it is people do with the leftovers of the dead. He doubted it. Juanita was still nearly hysterical with grief. And Willie was just too damn lazy to have done anything.

Third, would be to find anything relevant or of value. After all, he didn't know what he was looking for and he might not know if he found it. He wasn't trained or skilled at searching for evidence. Still, he clung to a faint feeling of optimism. Or was it excitement?

Last, would be escaping undetected. He didn't know if he could but he wasn't particularly afraid. He knew and Sacco knew, this was something he had to do. It wasn't a matter of choice.

He silently swung from his bike and set it down gently in some long grass just off the Lother property line. The house was an older, three-bedroom ranch-style that sat back a little way from the road in a veil of Ponderosa pines. There were no immediate neighbors. While the land directly on Loon Lake was fully developed, the secondary lots like this one weren't. And fortunately for Jess, the outside light that had been left on did little to make his presence obvious. After one in the morning, Jess didn't fear the lights from car traffic either. But he carefully stalked the perimeter of the property just to make sure of his surroundings. Then, after a few more minutes of silent observation, he casually walked up to the front door, reached under the porch, found and lifted the extra key, slipped it into the lock and let himself in.

"Hello," he called out in a disguised voice. "Anyone home?" His voice seemed to thunder in the dead stillness of the night. He was prepared to catapult out the front door at the slightest sound. None came.

It was dark inside, dark as the night outside and Jess allowed himself a few minutes for his pupils to dilate and adjust. His night vision was good but for some reason, he could not help thinking about a time, years ago, when he gazed through the sights of a Starlight Scope attached to his M-16 rifle. The scope electronically magnified light up to 50,000 times and through it, he saw objects in nearly pitch black from 400 yards away. He often asked himself why that one picture, of looking through the scope, out of all the pictures from that war tucked away in the recesses of his mind, came back so often. It was a question without an answer.

Through the curtain, the outside light seemed to grow brighter in time. And he noticed an indirect glow coming from the kitchen, probably an oven light.

Jess knew the simple layout of the house having been there once before. He was standing in the living room. Ahead and to his left were the eating area and a door to the garage. Straight ahead was the kitchen. Ahead and to the right was the hallway to the three bedrooms. The sole bathroom of the house would be on the left as was Willie and Juanita's room. Little Gloria's room was directly at the end of the hall and Gary's bedroom would be the first door on the right.

After a few more minutes of complete stillness, Jess removed a small flashlight from his pocket and turned it on with his hand over the end. He pointed it down at the floor and moved the few steps across the living room and around the corner to the hall. Gary's door was closed.

"Of course," he whispered. Juanita wouldn't want to look in at a thousand painful reminders every day.

Jess sucked in his breath and opened the door quickly.

He slowly guided the flashlight beam around the room and was surprised at what he saw. Gary's possessions were not only still there, it looked as though he might return any moment. Nothing appeared to have been touched at all.

The closet doors were open and dirty clothes were sitting on the floor in disorderly piles. The walls were lined with posters. One was a beautiful, full color picture of one of Gary's beloved loons, this one just breaking free of the water's surface. The bird's sharp beak was tucked tightly into its throat and the black crown of feathers was in striking contrast to the white design on its neck and back. The eyes shined a bright translucent blood red. Underneath it said "Common Loon" in large bold letters and underneath that, in parenthesis, was written "Gavia immer", the scientific name for the kind of loons found in that area.

Another poster was more typically adolescent. A tall, comely blonde woman in short shorts with a fully unbuttoned denim shirt and a provocatively arched back entreated the reader to sample some brand of beer. A third poster was a black and white blowup of a slightly fuzzy photograph of Gary taking a difficult hill on his motorcycle. Jess wondered who had taken the original picture since the boy's dad had no interest in this or any other hobby of Gary's.

Four shoes were on the floor, no two of which seemed to match. Next to the unmade bed was a homemade desk, an old door core set on two saw horses. The "desk" was as cluttered and messy as the rest of the room. But Jess could make out a clock radio and a boom box, an absolute membership requirement in teenage America. He also spotted two books: **Sand County Almanac** by Aldo Leopold and the other, **The Loon, Voice of the Wilderness** by Joan Dunning.

As Jess held the books he was nearly overcome by a powerful feeling almost like claustrophobia. "God, this room is tiny," he whispered to no one. It was cramped and cluttered. The whole room could fit in Jess' walk-in closet and the whole house was smaller than any one floor of his spacious new home. While it wasn't hot in the room, it was stifling; the air was stale and old. Jess stood motionless and concentrated on his breathing.

His eyes burned and then teared and the salty water ran down his face and into the corners of his mouth. He felt as though he would swoon and then he felt guilt, a deep physical guilt. Here he was, trespassing on Gary Lother's privacy. Looking at, touching and handling Gary's possessions, his treasures, the things that helped define who he was and what he cared about. Gary would never know, but that made Jess feel worse. It showed so little respect for someone that Jess knew had not received much in his short life.

The guilt gave way to pain as Jess' feelings began involuntarily to boil. His pain was grief, the primal form, the kind that comes from deep within and often manifests itself in a shattering and uncontrolled scream.

The agony of Gary's death racked him. This sad young boy with so much potential and so little help in life to realize it. A great sin had been committed by his premature death. A crime had been inflicted – not against laws or the state – but against all humanity. It had been robbed, not of a mere possession, but of a never ending genetic tributary that would flow throughout the ages. Of love, kindness, sensitivity, and happiness. And yes, of struggle and pain. Gone, prematurely extinguished before it was lit. Gone before it could create its own wake in the generations yet to come. Its weight so light upon the sands of time, that it had no chance to leave a footprint.

Suddenly, the room was bright as light shined through

the curtains from a car turning down the road. But it was enough to shake Jess out of his painful turmoil and bring him back to the task at hand. He wiped his face dry of tears and gently placed the books back on the desk and set about the business at hand. Despite his lack of training, he had logically concluded upon a semi-professional approach to the job, sectoring off the tiny room and thoroughly examining each area. He reasoned that it was a task similar to searching for an object in the woods or to archeology. You create multiple finite spaces and exhaust each one in its entirety before moving on to the next one. Closet bottom, clothes in closet, closet shelves. Desk top, desk drawer one, two, three, etc.

Jess found the first object of real interest under the bed at precisely the same time that he heard the noise. It was a snapping sound like a small branch being stepped on. It wasn't loud but it was distinguishable and close. Maybe just outside the window. Jess was lying on his stomach with his head under the bed when he heard it and he froze in that position. Could it have been an animal such as a dog or one of the many local porcupines? Not likely. The branch made too much noise for that and besides, there had been no noise since. Nothing. It was as though whatever or whoever was out there had frozen at the same instant.

Jess remembered the car lights. Perhaps it was a member of the Stevens County Emergency Search and Rescue team that advertised patrolling the homes around Loon Lake, but Jess doubted that. In all the years he had been coming to the lake, he had never seen a Stevens County ESAR team member or vehicle. Perhaps the lights he saw earlier had been someone parking down the road for their own midnight intrusion into the Lother home. A burglar? How would he know the Lothers were not home? But if it was, had he heard Jess?

Jess didn't wait for an answer to the question; he acted on instinct. He pushed himself up from the bed and walked over and turned the overhead light on. Then he stepped into the hall and quickly turned on the hall light. Immediately, he heard the sound of running footsteps rapidly receding into the night. Shortly thereafter came the sound of a nearby car being started and peeling out in the gravel. "One thing's for sure," Jess muttered to himself. "Whoever it was, wasn't supposed to be here anymore than I was."

He turned the hall and bedroom lights off, reached under the bed and grabbed the object and promptly walked out of the house. Thus far, he had been lucky. But there was no point in pressing his luck.

*　　*　　*

It was past four AM by the time Jess arrived home and settled down with a cup of fresh coffee on the main floor deck. He absentmindedly fiddled with his find while awaiting sunrise. He didn't yet want to go upstairs to shower for fear of waking Sacco. It was an unnecessary precaution as she slid through the door already dressed in her running clothes.

"How about the long course today, Gumbah?" she asked cheerfully.

"It's a little early, don't you think? In fact, it's a lot early. Besides, I'm tired."

"You don't think cavorting around all night is going to get you out of this, do you?"

"It doesn't seem like too much to hope for, now that you mention it."

She sat down on the outdoor love seat next to him with her bare thigh touching his. They both gazed at the lake and drank their coffee. It was the time before dawn when the light had not yet begun to change, when the morning birds were still sleeping. It was the in between time – not night and yet, still not morning.

"I have a feeling it's going to be a beautiful sunrise," she said.

He ignored her.

"Say, did you ever find out what the Spokane's call Loon Lake?"

"Nope. I called the tribal office. The person I spoke to didn't know. He said he would try to find out and call me back."

"I see."

They let several more minutes pass without conversation as the lake began to lighten with the first hint of sun and life. Their silence was a form of teasing and playfulness. He was seeing how long she could go before asking him how the breaking and entering had gone. She was waiting to see how long he could go without telling her. As usual, she won. It was unfair to compete in a test of wills with someone who made her living by dealing with teenagers, he would often say.

""Do you know what this is?" he asked, holding up the small glass object he had taken from underneath Gary Lother's bed.

"Sure. Do you?"

"No. Haven't the slightest."

"Then why did you steal it?"

"I'll tell you why I took it if you will tell me what it is."

"**And** if you will go running with me," she added.

"You drive a hard bargain."

"It's a reflux condenser tube."

"A reflex condenser?" he asked quizzically.

"No, a **reflux** condenser," she corrected.

"How do you know that?"

"You're not keeping your end of the bargain."

"See this tag on it down here? This is Gary's hand-writing. It says 'Found. 8-22.'"

"So?" she asked.

"Your turn," he insisted.

"Reflux condenser tubes are found in high school chemistry labs. They are used for certain experiments. I happen to know because I just approved purchasing a couple before school started." She raised one eyebrow inviting his response.

"August 22nd was the day before Gary was murdered."

CHAPTER NINE

Tommy wore a traditional blue, pinstriped suit in a fine blended wool. With it, he wore a pale blue, long-sleeved shirt with buttons, no cuff links, and a slightly loud paisley tie that was the new-old fashion. The tie's basic color scheme was red. For shoes, he wore the expensive cordovan Bostonians.

This was one of the ten basic "costumes" he owned. Big Brother called it Standard Businessman. Each time he traveled he wore a different costume. No two were similar. Nor were they particularly distinctive or eye-grabbing.

He had his Professor costume – slacks, casual dress shoes, a wool tweed sport coat and a heavy wool sweater. His slightly Bohemian costume. His Casual Slacks-Sports Shirt-Blue Blazer-and Topsiders costume. His Hawaiian Vacation costume. And so forth.

He wore a different one each week he took the trip to Los Angeles. Big Brother insisted.

For his weekly trips he even shaved and combed his stringy hair. Somehow it made his deep-set eyes seem less so, and less blue than their normal color.

He alternated flying out of Spokane and Seattle. Another requirement of Big Brother. Occasionally he would even drive all the way down to Boise for the flight out. He never returned through the city of origin either. He paid cash for each flight and used a different name every time.

He enjoyed making up names or borrowing them. He and Big Brother would do this on the night before his departure. A couple of times he used the names of friends from Vietnam who had died. Sometimes he bastardized famous names. Dan Jennings on the way down. Peter Rather on the way back. Or he would play with names from books or movie stars. L. Marvin for Lee Marvin. Or Larry Sanders for Lawrence Sanders, the popular mystery writer. The names were never too cute or noticeable, however.

Today he was leaving from Spokane as a Mr. Bill Bennett. He took Delta Flight #1249 to LAX. Strictly coach class. Always coach. Something he never told Big Brother about were the conversations he had with other passengers on his flights. He invented complete identities for himself of interesting and happy people. He tried hard not to make them too interesting, though. There were just too many suspicious people around. He knew enough – Big Brother had told him a thousand times – not to want to be remembered. It was important that no one be able to describe him accurately. That is why he wore the different costumes. So no one would notice, even over a period of many months, that he had been at any given airport several times. Anonymity was the key to his protection against all those suspicious people.

When he landed at the Los Angeles airport, he took the hotel van after retrieving his one checked suitcase. He registered at the Hyatt Regency as a Mr. Martin, paid cash in advance for a one night stay and was assigned to Room 1507. He went straight there after politely refusing any help from the Bell Captain. He only had two bags; one was a small carry-on and the other was the large, heavy suitcase he had checked at baggage.

He placed the larger bag under the queen sized bed and immediately left the room with the carry-on bag over his shoulder. On the way out, he took a roll of duct tape, checked the hall for other guests, and taped over the locking mechanism so that it would open for whoever pushed on the door. He also put out the "Do Not Disturb" sign so the house maid wouldn't come in to turn his bed down and leave those stupid little chocolate candies on his pillow. He went downstairs to the lobby to a pay phone, inserted a quarter and dialed.

"Hello," the voice answered.

"The Hyatt Regency. Room 1507," he responded. "Now repeat it to me."

"The Hyatt Regency. Room 1507."

He hung up, walked out the back entrance of the hotel, down the street three blocks to a Holiday Inn and registered at the front desk as a Robert Thurow. He paid cash. All according to the plan he and Big Brother had worked out. In his room, he unfolded a change of clothes from his carry-on bag and hung them in the closet. He then went down stairs to the dining room where he had a light dinner. Afterwards, he returned to his room and watched television for an hour before turning out the light and falling asleep.

Tommy woke early the next morning and showered, shaved and dressed. Back at the Hyatt, he let himself into his room using the key since the duct tape had been removed in the middle of the night. He reached under the bed, pulled out the dark suitcase that looked identical to the one he left there the day before and opened it. Tommy smiled a deep smile of satisfaction. He didn't bother counting the money. He knew it would be exactly $800,000 in unmarked twenties and fifties.

He placed the key on the night stand and left the room with his carry-on bag and the replacement luggage. He took the hotel van back to the airport and booked a flight to Seattle using yet another name and paying cash.

Same thing. Week in and week out.

CHAPTER TEN

The next day, Jess fulfilled his promise to guest lecture at the high school. The young teacher who had asked him at the faculty party, called to remind him of his promise just prior to school's starting. After trying several lame excuses to get out of the commitment, Jess relented. He never suspected the conspiracy between Sacco and the teacher to try to get him more involved with people and out of the house. Their easy manipulation of him succeeded where highly paid lobbyists had failed for years; maybe their cause was nobler.

By the time first lunch break arrived, Jess was physically exhausted. All morning long he performed as much as he "taught." And it took a great deal of energy.

His objective was to bring to life the "dance of legislation" that he always found so exciting, dramatic and worthwhile; and that many people found so boring, venal and arcane.

He plopped down in the chair across from Sacco's desk while she continued a telephone conversation. She silently mouthed "just a minute." Reading the weariness in his face, she smiled and gave him a sympathetic look and a wink.

He half listened to the conversation she was having

with an obviously irate parent. Some days, having these kinds of conversations was all Sacco got done. Occasionally, parents were justified in their irritation and Sacco was the first to admit, privately, that the system and some of its employees had a shocking proclivity for insensitivity and bureaucratic non-think. But more often, the parents automatically took their child's side regardless of evidence and common sense.

Just now, Sacco was explaining appeal rights to a parent who was arguing that a long-term suspension of his sophomore son was excessive. The student had been found with a twenty-two caliber pistol and a box of shells in his locker. Jess marveled at how unemotional and almost soothing Sacco was.

She cradled the phone with a small sigh and turned to Jess with a slight grin. "Well, not used to making an honest living, huh?"

"Good lord, paisan, I felt like a student teacher again. Everything I did fell flat. Even my jokes. I felt like I was working with a class of zombies. I told our young friend I would have to come back another time to catch his afternoon classes. Frankly, I don't think he was sorry I didn't stay."

"Well, it isn't exactly like riding a bike. Besides, you were just visiting. That's barely a notch above substituting which is the closest thing to hell on earth yet invented." She paused and lowered her voice. "Maybe you weren't ready, Gumbah. After all, you didn't really want to do this."

"You're right. I had an ulterior motive."

"Having lunch with me," she grinned.

"Uh, well, not exactly," he offered guiltily.

"I'm hurt," she feigned, clutching her hand over her heart.

"I was hoping to talk to Barney Rubble."

She understood immediately. "Ahhh. You wanted to talk to him about the reflux condenser tube. Well, your timing is good. This is his planning period and he's in his room. 213. Unlike some, you'll find him working."

He rose slowly from his place of rest and leaned over the desk. He caressed her cheek with the back of his fingers and whispered, "Don't be late this afternoon. I feel my energy returning already, surging, as it were, in my, ahem, veins."

"Mmmm, such big talk," she cooed. "You can't outrun me and you can't–"

"One way to find out," he interrupted. "And I can guarantee it will be a fun discovery."

"I've told you a hundred million times not to exaggerate. Room 213, Big Talker. See you this afternoon." He kissed her quickly and softly on the lips, turned on his heels and left.

In the second wing of the small high school he found the room and walked in. Barney Rubble stood behind a counter at the front of the room, the school's one general purpose science room. In here, Barney, who hadn't noticed Jess come in, taught three periods of biology to sophomores and two periods of chemistry to juniors. After school, he was the adviser to the Future Farmers of America (FFA) program. His work with students in FFA had won him nearly every teaching and community award imaginable. Despite his conservative ways and seeming lack of personality, he managed to develop many students that all others had lost hope for. The only answer for his unusual success was the obvious one: he was a hard-working, well organized teacher with high expectations for his students regardless of what they or others thought of them. And what he expected, he got.

Barney struck a peculiar out-of-place-and-time figure. His crew cut and large features made his head seem even larger than it was. He was short and stocky and looked strong with a rugged, weather-worn face. His clothing was always conventional and out of fashion. Today he wore a white short-sleeved shirt with button down collar and gray slacks. He had on a plain red tie. He also owned a blue one. Behind the door to the storage room hung his brown corduroy jacket. It was the only sport coat he owned.

The room itself was much more interesting looking than the man. One entire counter top was covered with the cages of exotic looking reptiles. It also contained the obligatory paraphernalia for a science room from the periodic table of elements to various stuffed animals. Barney taught a course on taxidermy as part of FFA and some of his own work was displayed here. This included the heads of a bear and a moose as well as a full-sized deer. In some urban districts in Washington, such exhibits would have sparked protests from animal rights groups. In northeast Washington, it wasn't an issue. The only debate here was whether or not an NRA-taught course on gun safety should be a high school graduation requirement.

Jess was struck by how clean and neat the room was. He recalled that when he was in high school, the science room was in a state of constant physical chaos. For that matter, so was every science room in every building in which he had taught. What they all had in common with this one, however, were the smells. Here he sensed a familiar combination of formaldehyde and the sweet smell of the burner gas used in so many experiments. Jess' sense of smell was acute, sometimes painfully so. In Vietnam he would occasionally vomit around death – not at its sight but at its smell.

The second time he cleared his throat Barney finally looked up from his intense concentration.

"Mr. Speaker," he said self-consciously, "sorry I didn't

see you. I heard you were in the building this morning. To what do I owe this honor?" Barney came around the counter talking and extending his hand as he went.

"I'm looking for help from the school's finest science teacher."

Barney either didn't get the joke or didn't think it was funny.

"Sure. Sure. Anything I can do."

Jess held up the reflux condenser he had retrieved from his car. "Can you tell me how this might be used?"

"It's a reflux condenser tube."

"Yes, I know. Sacco told me that much. But what I want to know is what they are used for."

"I don't know what this one is used for. We have a couple that we use in experiments. Ours are slightly larger versions of this one."

"What kind of experiments?"

"Well, it could be anything where you want to vaporize a material and then condense it or solidify it back again."

"Such as?"

"Gosh, it could be anything. Here we do a thing where we cook wood fiber." He took the tube in his hands and pointed. "The wood fiber is cooked and vaporizes up the middle tube here, the tube within a tube. Cool water is circulated down the outside tube here. Then at the top, the vapor liquefies and comes out this outlet and into another container. Then we examine the reconstructed materials."

Jess thought for a moment. "A wood experiment. Is that all?"

"Yes, here that is. Actually, we only do it as part of a unit relating to the forest products industry. Lots of students come from families that work in the woods or at a mill. And we probably wouldn't even do that except the industry people give us a grant once a year."

Jess was feeling frustrated. "How else, Barney? How

else could one of these be used?"

"Well, like I say, just about any number of ways where you wanted to cook and mix materials as gas and then condense them."

Science was not Jess' forte and never had been. In high school, college and graduate school, he had avoided the sciences and their labs as much as possible. He could not relate to what Barney was saying and it felt like someone was talking to him in a foreign language he didn't understand. He tried a different tack. "Where do you get these, Barney?"

"I order them out of a catalogue. That is, with your wife's approval."

"That's the only way they are available? Out of a catalogue?"

"No, I suppose you could buy one at a supply house. At school, it's easier and cheaper to buy them out of the catalogue along with other supplies. But like I say, they aren't that big an item in high schools. Least not here." He handed the tube back to Jess. "I don't know if I helped you, Mr. Speaker, but then again, I'm not sure what you are looking for."

"I'm sorry, Barney. I never did explain myself. Did you know the Lother boy? The one they say drowned?"

"Just by sight. I would have though. He was scheduled to take biology from me this quarter. That was real sad. It is any time a young person dies. What's the connection?"

"This tube was found by the Lother boy the day before he died. He thought enough of it to label it and date it. And I am at a loss, Barney. Do you have any ideas why a kid would have something like this?"

Barney rubbed his chin and thought. "No," he said slowly. "I really don't. The boy wouldn't even have had chemistry for another year. And he didn't have a big brother or sister. Beats me."

"Well, thanks, anyway. I appreciate your time."

"You're welcome to my time, Jess, but I don't know how much help I've been. I tell you what, though, I'll thumb through some experiment books and see if I can come up with an idea or two about why he might have had the tube. Okay?"

"Thanks again, Barney." Jess turned to leave but stopped at the door. "By the way, is there a supply house that sells these around here?"

"No, there isn't. They wouldn't do enough volume to carry it."

"How about in Spokane?"

"Now that you mention it, I think there is."

"Do you remember the name?"

"Let me see, it's, uh, Inland Empire Chemical Supply. That's it," he said snapping his fingers at the same time. "I think it's out on Trent, a little ways east of downtown."

"Thanks, Barney. You really have been a help."

Jess left thinking to himself, "Two steps forward, one step backward." He wasn't sure he would make it home for his appointed tryst or not. He had something else in mind now.

CHAPTER ELEVEN

Jess left the high school parking lot and drove straight for Spokane on Highway 395, trying to formulate a plan in his mind as he went. A rare shortage of the normally traffic-slowing farm trucks on the two lane highway reduced the drive to town to a quick 30 minutes. All around him, sunshine lit up the green and gold fields of the farms and pastures and brightened his mood, making it difficult for him to concentrate.

Just north of Spokane, Highway 395 became North Division Street and led the last several miles to downtown through seemingly hundreds of stoplights which were synchronized to require stopping at every block. It always frustrated Jess that this leg of the trip to downtown Spokane often took as much time as the first thirty miles to the edge of town.

The north side of Spokane had grown rambunctiously over the last several years with both sides of Division packed with restaurants, movie theaters, and retail outlets of all kinds. Halfway into town was Northtown, a massive indoor mall, whose potential had been fully appreciated and developed by an aggressive young businessman from Seattle.

Finally, Division crossed the Spokane River into the

unofficial beginning of downtown. To the west was Spokane Falls Boulevard and to the east was Trent Avenue – the same street with two different names. The western and more commercial downtown portion had been renamed during the Expo '76 celebration many years before. Expo sparked a profound community pride as well as an escalation in property values. Small fortunes had been made by those brave or lucky enough to own property in a skid row area that was suddenly surrounded by the Opera House, a convention center, new hotels and restaurants and a refurbished park on the river. The former residents were absorbed into less visible parts of the community.

Even before Expo, Spokane was a beautiful town, with its impressive neighborhoods and stately houses, especially on the South Hill where most of the city's economic elite live and where the great mining and timber wealthy of the past built their mansions, huge houses with massive turnaround driveways and imposing columns. Virtually every corner of town has some pocket of housing with the kind of views that cost fortunes to own in most cities, views of distant mountains or sharp gorge-like valleys. Only in the Spokane Valley to the east is there the look and feel of traditional suburbanization. There, rapid growth has been fueled by businesses seeking a higher quality of life for their employees but lower expectations about wages.

Spokane is a fiercely proud town, proud of its frequent awards as one of the most livable cities in America and of its role as the center of commerce and culture for all eastern Washington and northern Idaho. It is big enough to occasionally draw big name talent for its Opera Center, to have several local television stations, and to have a real downtown with a real skyline – the only one for well over a hundred miles. Its identity is built upon its frontier origins, its cleanliness (except for the irregular air pollution problems), and its perpetual concern about being left out or behind by its much bigger sister city to the west, Seattle.

Jess loved the town and loved visiting it. He said it was "emotionally navigable" and never left him feeling intimidated or lost or overwhelmed like larger and less friendly cities did.

But what he loved most about the town and the whole area, including the lake, was its climate. Hot summers. Crisp falls. Cold, snowy winters. And striking springs. Distinct seasons each with a vivid personality and feel of their own. It was a total contrast to his previous home west of the Cascades – or on "the coast" as people in Spokane would say even though he was no where near the Pacific Ocean – where there was only one season: Gray, the gray of constant rain. More than fifty inches a year. There was a saying in his home town: if you could see Mt. Rainier in the distance, it meant it was going to rain within 24 hours; if you couldn't, it was because it was already raining.

He circled around the block so he could turn east on Trent, away from the downtown and toward the chemical supply company and through an older section of Spokane, one that had escaped unscathed from any urban renewal efforts. It was older and more tired than most of Spokane with its mix of weedy vacant lots and mostly wholesale businesses. One retail exception was an Italian deli and grocery store popular for its fine imports and food. Sacco often brought home specially made sausage from the septuagenarian immigrant owner. She talked a little Italian to him and he smiled and flirted a lot with her.

Jess looked both ways before doing a U-turn to park in front of the Inland Empire Chemical Supply Company.

The building, concrete block construction with copious coats of paint that had no color, fit right into the neighborhood. It had a storefront window display, single front door entrance and a small attached warehouse. A long sign over the window named the business in faded letters. The window display featured home chemistry sets for high schoolers that looked as if they were manufactured in response to the Sputnik threat.

Jess casually looked around the neighborhood at its other businesses and vacant lots, still trying to formulate a plan in his mind. He didn't have one but he walked in the front door anyway hoping inspiration would strike any second.

The inside of Inland Empire Chemical was as tired as the outside, drab and out of date. A single Formica top counter separated the customer from the employee area. The space in front of the counter was small and there were no chairs, not even the old vinyl kind with metal arms and big full ashtrays next to them. The floor was a linoleum with a circa 1950's design. The walls were paneled and decorated with a single "starving artist" seascape and a lone clock with a cord that hung down the wall to the outlet.

Behind the counter and to the right was an open door to the warehouse where neat stacks of cans, cartons and barrels were visible. Against the back wall stood a long row of ante bellum filing cabinets. In front of these sat an old, metal desk with a phone and calculator on top amidst endless piles of invoice-looking papers.

Also behind the counter stood Tim, so identified by the name tag over his right shirt pocket. Tim weighed too much, about fifty pounds too much for his medium height. The extra weight gave his face, with its crown of short red hair and map of freckles, a slightly bloated look. He didn't bother to look up at Jess or offer the obligatory

"I'll be with you in a minute." Instead, he went on helping the only other customer present.

"Let me confirm. Two pounds of phenyl acetic acid and one gallon of ether. Correct?" Tim asked. The customer nodded.

"Be right back," Tim offered as he departed through the warehouse door. Jess took measure of the man, who was looking at something on top of the counter, without feeling self-conscious. He was tall and thin with a tiny gold earring in his left earlobe and a long pony tail of dark brown hair. His sharp features were accented by a long mustache. Several gold chains hung loose across his neck, visible in the open collar shirt unbuttoned halfway down his sparsely hairy chest. He wore a short, black leather jacket with tight blue jeans and had on a pair of expensive-looking snake skin cowboy boots. The flesh between his thumb and index finger was tattooed with an object that looked to Jess like a pair of wings.

Tim returned through the doorway carrying a gallon can that was marked "ether" and a small opaque, plastic jar which he promptly placed into a sack. As he entered the office, an unpleasant whiff of odor came with him that Jess thought was vaguely familiar. "Cat urine," he thought. "My god, they've got a brood of cats in back."

Tim handed an invoice to the customer who reached into his jeans, pulled out a bulging money clip and peeled off the appropriate number of bills. The exchange of money for product and paperwork all took place without conversation.

After the man left, Jess shuffled down the counter to stand in front of Tim who was filing the invoice. Without looking up he said, "Yes?" Not, "Yes, may I help you?" Jess knew then he should have spent more time on a plan.

Without thinking, he pulled the reflux condenser retrieved from the Lother house out of a paper sack and asked, "Do you sell these?"

"Yes. How many would you like?"

"Well, I don't actually want any. I just wanted to see if you sold them."

Tim just looked at Jess and Jess just felt foolish.

"Do you keep records of who you sell them to?"

"Whose asking and why?" Tim's voice was even and without hostility.

"Well, this is going to sound a little strange, Tim" – maybe familiarity would loosen him up – "but this condenser was found in the room of a boy who drowned and nobody seems to know why he might have had it. It seemed sort of out of place."

"I see." Tim looked almost thoughtful. "It's a reflux condenser. The boy was probably using it for high school chemistry."

"No. He didn't have chemistry yet."

"Well, can't help you then."

"Would you know if this was purchased here?"

"No. Reflux condensers don't have serial numbers."

"But you do keep track of purchases."

"Yes. But unless the purchase was on credit or by check for a large amount, we often don't even write the name down. No need to waste time."

Tim seemed to be overly concerned with efficiency of all effort.

"Isn't there a way you could check and see how many of this kind of reflux condensers you sold in the last several months?"

"Could. But I won't. We do hundreds of transactions a month. Everything from chlorine to cleaning agents. No idea where to start."

"I see . . ." Jess' voice trailed off as he struggled to think of some way to enlist Tim in his cause.

"You a cop or something?" Tim deadpanned. His expression never changed. Jess wondered why none of his facial muscles ever moved when he spoke.

"No. Just trying to make sense of something is all."

"Can't help you." It was the second time Tim had said it and Jess was beginning to believe him.

Jess fiddled with the condenser a little while longer and mulled the circumstance over. "Dead end," he thought.

"Thank you for your time," he said as he turned to leave. Tim managed a grunt.

*   *   *

Jess let the automatic garage door close behind him as he parked his car in the massive four-car garage. He thought he would be home in time for dinner but found nothing in the oven and no one in the house. Finally, he saw Sacco in the hot tub through the basement window. He shed all his clothes, walked onto the patio and slipped into the hot tub with her. She sat facing the lake and sipping on a glass of white wine. She did not acknowledge his presence in anyway even with eye contact. He sat looking at her and thinking.

"I asked you to be home early, didn't I?" he offered with a highly apologetic tone to his voice. She said nothing. "And let me guess. You left work early even though you should have stayed because I asked and then I wasn't here. Right?"

"That's part of it." She still wasn't looking at him.

"Uh, and I got your hopes up about my fabulous love making?"

A slight smile quickly flashed across her eyes but not her lips; he missed it. She had years of practice concealing mirth from goofy teenagers. "The polite thing to do would have been to leave a note. That doesn't take much effort. Or time." She said it as though angry and for all

Jess knew, she was.

"I'm sorry, paisan. You're right, of course. I drove down to Spokane to follow up on a tip that Barney gave me about the reflux condenser. I just didn't want to wait until tomorrow."

"Patience is not a flower that grows in your garden."

"You're right. Despite the fact that I think patience is an over-rated virtue, what I did wasn't very thoughtful. How can I make it up to you?" He sounded genuinely sorry. "Can I make dinner tonight or have you eaten?"

She finally looked at him and seemed to melt just a little.

"That's a good start . . . but just a start."

"What else?"

"We have some unfinished business."

"Sure," he said smiling. "Dinner or dessert first?"

"Neither – yet. I want to hear about your day first. Woman does not live by bread – or cake – alone." She was finally herself as she floated across the hot tub to kiss him and sit next to him draping her naked thigh over his.

"Well, it was pretty disappointing. I went to a chemical supply company that sells reflux condensers. One that Barney told me about. They couldn't tell me if they had sold the one I found in Gary's room and he couldn't enlighten me as to why Gary might have had it or what he might have used it for. I didn't accomplish much except burn some gas and make myself chef for the evening."

"That's it?"

"That was it. The only memorable thing about the visit was the cat urine smell that darn near choked me."

"Is that what a chemical supply place smells like? I would've thought it would be more like chlorine or something clinical."

"I don't know. The smell came from something sold

to the customer ahead of me. It was fairly strong but I was thinking how much the guy reminded me of you."

"Does it come as a surprise that sometimes you make next to no sense whatsoever?"

"Well, you see, the customer ahead of me had a tattoo of wings or something on his hand." Jess pointed to the spot. "And I was thinking about the cute little butterfly tattoo on that great ass of yours." He grinned mischievously. She had been tattooed when he dared her years ago that she wouldn't; it cured him of making dares forever.

"The wing tattoo in that spot is probably a gang marking, Jess." Sacco had had many run-ins with gang activity through the years. Too many to take it lightly. "Did the wings look like the symbol for a Harley Davidson motorcycle?"

"Now that you mention it, yes."

"No doubt a gang marking then. Was he wearing any colors?"

"No, not at all. He had on jeans and an open sport shirt and a nice leather jacket. For god's sake, he had cowboy boots on. Gang members don't wear cowboy boots, do they?"

"They do in Texas." She was kidding but he didn't get it. "Notice anything else about him?" she continued.

"Well, he did pay with a Texas-size wad of bills."

"What did you say he bought?"

"I don't know. There were two things. I can only say that at least one of them smelled like the wet end of a cat box. Why?"

"I don't know, Jess. You feel like you came up empty. I think you ought to talk to Sheriff Page."

"So he can arrest me for breaking and entering the Lother's? What are you trying to do, get rid of me?" He was trying to be light-hearted but she wasn't.

"Look, Jess," – time to sit up straight, he thought – "I've stuck with you on this thing despite some doubts. Even when you made your midnight burglary. I think I know what this means to you. But if, just if, you're on to something here, you need not to be doing a Lone Ranger deal." She paused and in a way that suggested there was no option, added, "It is a reasonable expectation on my part."

They sat in silence for several minutes.

"Okay," he said with resignation. "What do you want for dinner?"

"I want dessert first."

They got out of the hot tub and toweled one another dry in the basement and walked the two flights up to their bedroom and giant bed hand in hand. Their love making was soft and gentle and lasted a delightfully long time. By the time they finally sat down to dinner hours later, both were famished.

CHAPTER TWELVE

Jess made good on his word the next day by phoning Sheriff Bill Page up and inviting him over to dinner. Jess pretended it was just social and Page pretended to believe him but the truth was both men had different agendas.

That evening, they sat on the deck enjoying the lake and drinking expensive Starbuck's blend coffee together while Sacco finished preparing the meal. The lake was smooth and quiet and the temperature was in the mid-seventies. It was shirt sleeve weather. Even the straight-laced Sheriff was out of uniform and looking comfortable in a pair of cotton slacks and a polo shirt. Jess doubted the man owned a pair of old blue jeans or a sweat shirt.

They made small talk about the lake, the Sheriff's work and a little on local politics until Sacco walked out and announced that dinner was ready. Both men quickly helped to bring the dishes out to the expensive outdoor dining table.

"This looks great, Sacco," the Sheriff said. "I don't get enough home cooked meals." It was as close as the stoic man would ever come to acknowledging the painful divorce of several years ago. His wife had suddenly left him for another man in Spokane. Page came home from work late one night to find her closets and drawers empty and a note taped to the oven. It was what she did with the years of stress, accumulated from being married to someone in law enforcement, not knowing what tragedy the next phone call might bring or how close to home it might hit. Her new husband was a successful real estate agent in the valley to the east of Spokane.

"Indeed, paisan, you've outdone yourself," Jess added.

It was Sacco's favorite meal to prepare and eat – lasagna with ample, layered dosages of ricotta, mozzarella, sauce with sausage from the Spokane deli, and huge pasta noodles, all served with a light salad and steamy French bread with real butter. Jess remembered when real butter was a luxury in their household.

The small talk continued for a while with Sacco joining in with her own stories about school. Both men contributed to the stall while trying to figure out how to broach their respective subjects with some natural segue.

Finally, after the plates had been cleared and Sacco was setting small bowls of fruit in front of them, Jess asked, "Bill, do you know what a reflux condenser is?" It wasn't particularly smooth but it was time to get down to business.

"It's a piece of glassware used in labs. Why do you ask?"

"Well, suppose, Bill, suppose that one was found in Gary Lother's room and there seemed to be no reason for it to be there. He hadn't taken chemistry at school yet, had no other chemistry equipment at home or anything. Would that suggest anything to you?"

"Besides questions about how it was obtained?"

"Yeah. Does it?"

"I don't have enough information. Kids pick up things all the time and make treasures of them."

"What if it was tagged? What if it said 'Found? 8-22.'? That was the day before Gary was found dead. Drowned according to you. The victim of foul play according to me."

"Drowned according to the medical examiner, Jess," the Sheriff corrected. Now they were getting to his reason for accepting Jess' dinner invitation. He wanted to know if Jess had acted on his belief that the Lother boy had been murdered. "It's still not enough to go on by a long shot. It's not even enough to get started on."

Jess had the feeling that Bill was thinking something and not saying it.

"You're telling me," Jess responded dejectedly.

Sacco took over. "And what would you say, Bill, if the reflux condenser was taken to a chemical supply company in Spokane where it very well might have been purchased and something a little suspicious was observed?"

"Such as?"

"Such as a cash transaction by someone who did **not** look like they were buying cleaning agents," she added.

"Go on."

"Carrying the tattoo sign of gang membership."

"That's it? A 'suspicious' looking character pays cash for you-know-not-what at a business where a piece of glass found in Gary Lother's house **might** have been purchased? And you want to know what it might mean?"

Jess and Sacco looked at one another tentatively.

"Is that it? That's all?"

"Well," Jess added almost sheepishly, "There was a strong smell of something like cat urine." Then he hastily added the hypothetical, "I mean, what **if** there was a smell like cat urine?"

Even the normally sober Sheriff could not conceal the momentary look in his eyes but he quickly recovered. "I think what we have here is an open and shut case of over-active imagination. Nothing more. Nothing less." The Sheriff said it with finality.

Jess and Sacco sat uncomfortably and sipped on their coffee. Jess was unconvinced by the Sheriff's dismissal and Sacco was feeling guilty for having insisted to Jess that he involve the Sheriff. The silence was eventually broken by the distant sound of a loon.

"What's that, Jess?" she asked, trying to change the subject.

"It's The Yodel."

"It's my favorite," she added just as they heard another Yodel, the song of the loon. It was a slow rising note followed by quick undulating phrases. "What does it signify?"

Jess recalled his lessons from Gary Lother well. "It can mean simple identification between birds or it might be a cry of territorial defense." Jess wondered to himself if Bill was defending his territory that evening.

He didn't wonder long as his thoughts were interrupted by a loud blast of the local volunteer fire department's siren. The station was located just across Highway 395, less than a mile from where they sat. It was so intrusive as to prohibit further conversation.

"May I use your phone? I think I'll just check on that," Bill said loud enough to be heard.

Sacco nodded, got up and gestured for the Sheriff to follow her into the house to a phone. A few minutes later he returned. During an interim of horn blasts, he said, "Against my better judgment, Jess, you may want to come with me. That alarm is for a house fire down the road. It's the Lothers."

*   *   *

It was only a few minutes later that Jess and the Sheriff pulled up to the Lother house one mile away and back off the lake. The local full-time fire chief was already on hand as well as eight volunteers, scrambling to and fro under his command. They were working with one fire truck and two water tankers. People from around the lake were beginning to assemble and watch the blaze.

"Too late," the Sheriff observed. "It will be a complete loss."

"You sure?"

"Yes. The fire reached flashover before the crew could get here. What a shame. Even though the station is just down the road, the added time of volunteers getting to the station was probably all it took."

"What do you mean 'flashover', Bill?"

"The point at which the heat in the room is high enough to ignite its contents. You know, 451 degrees Fahrenheit, like in the movie. When that happens, and it only takes a few minutes if the fire is going good and the windows are open and feeding it, it's likely to be pretty much of a total loss. Look there." He pointed to the house. "Most of those windows are open at least partially. That's worse than pouring gasoline on to a fire."

Jess didn't say so just then, but he didn't remember the windows being open the other evening when he was in the Lother house.

The Sheriff left to check with the fire chief during a brief break in instructions and Jess was joined by irascible Ben from Granite Point who had been one of the first people on the scene.

"Anybody in there, Ben?" Jess asked.

"Nope. Don't think so. They're still down at Juanita's family in Oregon." After a pause, he added, "Think I will find out who knows the number down there. Someone ought to give them a call." Underneath his gruff exterior, Ben was a thoughtful soul. He just didn't tolerate fools very well.

Jess offered to make himself useful but was politely

told things were well in hand and please, just stand back. He watched with fascination as part of the crew rapidly brought the house fire, which fully enveloped the structure by the time he arrived, quickly under control. Another part of the crew was spraying white foam on the nearby branches of the surrounding Ponderosa pines. Plant life was still dry from the summer and if the fire got into the trees, it could spread quickly to the other houses even though an acre or more separated them from one another. The prospect wasn't lost on anyone and accounted for the keen attention of the spectators.

Ben strode back over after working the crowd for the Lother's specific whereabouts. Jess was sitting on the hood of the Sheriff's car taking in the drama which was coming to an amazingly fast conclusion.

"Any luck, Ben?"

"No number. Got a name and town, though. It should be easy enough to find a number and give them a call. Think I will wait until first thing in the morning. They couldn't do anything about it tonight. Too late to drive back up. Why worry them now?"

"With them gone, what do you suppose started it?" Jess asked out loud, even though he had his own suspicions. Just then, they were rejoined by the Sheriff who gratefully took a cup of coffee offered to him by Ben.

"Any ideas on what started it, Bill?" Jess asked.

"Yes. It was arson." He said it matter of factly and without emotion.

"How can you know that already?" The open flames of the fire were now fully extinguished and the crew was doing the "knockdown", walking through the house and applying light doses of water to any smoldering objects.

"The Chief has a good nose for this kind of situation. He's already been in the house with a Hydrocarbon Detector; you might also call it a flammable liquid detector.

Anyway, the Chief says the readings were very high. He thinks someone doused all the beds and furniture with some flammable substance – maybe even gasoline – and lit a match to it. Whoever did it was more concerned with burning the house down than hiding the fact that it was started on purpose."

"This probably supports the evidence, Bill, but I was, uh, by here the other night and I am pretty sure the windows were all closed at that time. Which stands to reason. I don't think anyone would leave for several days like the Lothers have and just leave their windows open."

"What kind of an idiot would do something like this, Sheriff?" Ben asked.

"It's hard to tell, Ben. The most common motivations for arson are insurance fraud or psychological perversion."

"But the Lothers are the insured ones and they aren't here. They probably would have lost as much as they gained anyway," Ben observed.

"Aren't you leaving a possibility out, Bill?" Jess asked.

"Such as?"

"Such as someone was trying to destroy incriminating contents, whatever that may be?"

"At this point, all possibilities are on the table. We don't have enough information to make an informed judgment." Jess had heard this line before from the Sheriff.

The three men drank their coffee in silence while the crew put the finishing touches on its job. The crowd soon dissipated and the fire fighters reloaded their hoses and equipment and returned to the station to debrief and relive their drama. The chief stayed for a few minutes in private conversation with the Sheriff before he, too, bid his farewell. Ben took this as his cue to "head for the barn."

When the last sound of Ben's old pickup had completely faded, Bill turned to Jess and said, "I think it's time you told me everything. Everything."

Jess looked up at him from his sitting position on the car hood and answered, "I really have, Bill. In fact, I was hoping you could tell me something. That's why I was asking you those questions at dinner."

"Everything, Jess?"

"Well, there is one thing. The night I was in the Lother house – which I am not really admitting to you – I heard someone right outside the window. That's why I am sure the windows were closed. I was right there looking through that window over there" – he pointed – " and it was closed then. Anyway, I started turning on lights and I heard someone running away. Then they got into a car and tore out of here."

The Sheriff pondered this information a while.

"Come on. Let's kick over a dirty burnt timber or two," he said as he headed for the house.

By now, there wasn't even any smoke left. It was just an eerie blackened shell of something several people once called home. Jess thought about how this tragedy might affect the already fragile Mrs. Lother. First, she lost her son. Now she lost her home and all its possessions. There probably wasn't anything of value in the home that wouldn't be covered by insurance. But it would be the mementos and keepsakes that would hurt. No doubt, every picture of her dead son had just gone up in smoke. When Mrs. Lother realized that she would have to rely exclusively on her mind and its progressively fainter images for remembrances of her son, she would be shattered. Jess feared for her mental well being.

"Show me where you found the reflux condenser," the Sheriff asked as they entered the house. Everything in sight was black, charcoaled by the flames.

Jess took him to Gary's bedroom and pointed to the

vestige of a bed. "It was under his bed. There, Bill. Just sitting there. Not wrapped up in a sack or anything. Except for being under the bed, there was no real effort to hide it."

Jess felt unsafe in the house as though the fire might spontaneously re-combust or he might fall through the floor. He stood still, hoping his silence would leave undisturbed whatever might haunt this space while the Sheriff made busy, poking around the blackened debris and lifting up objects here and there. If there was a method to his search, it escaped Jess.

"What's this?" Bill asked from the former closet. He was using a pencil to hold up the tiny ring handle of a door to the crawl space beneath the house. He took out a handkerchief and wrapped his fingers in it before reaching down and popping open the door revealing the dirt below and something else.

"Well, well. What have we here?"

He started to lift up a small metal box but quickly dropped it. "Ouch! Damn," he said, waving his hand, "the thing is still hot." He rewrapped his hand with the handkerchief and quickly lifted it out setting it on the floor. "Did you see this when you were here before, Jess?"

"No, I didn't. I was interrupted by the noise outside and left. I looked in the closet but the floor was covered with shoes and clothes and I didn't even see the door under the mess."

"It might be nothing."

The Sheriff used a pen from his pocket to spring open the door of the box which looked like a common change box used to hold cash and coins. When the lid opened, he reached in and tested the object inside to see how hot it was. Satisfied he wouldn't be burned, the Sheriff juggled it out and set it on the ground.

"What is it?" Jess asked anxiously. He was looking at

a small square metal object with an on/off switch and what appeared to be two hose connections. He had no idea what it was.

The Sheriff picked it up with the handkerchief and began slowly examining it.

"It's a vacuum pump."

"Yeah? So? So what? What's it for?"

"Just that, Jess. It's a little electric motor that creates a vacuum for certain lab work. Pure and simple. These connectors are where it attaches to other equipment."

"Like what?" Jess pressed.

"Oh, could be just about anything, really."

"Is this getting us anywhere, Bill?" Jess sounded impatient. He was feeling frustrated.

The Sheriff turned it over and was peering intently at the bottom of the pump. "I think we're getting somewhere now," he said with quiet discovery in his voice.

"What? What is it, damn it, Bill?"

Page quickly placed the pump back in the metal box and carefully picked it up and started for the car.

"Hey! Wait a minute, Bill. Damnit!" Jess shouted. "What the hell gives?"

Page stopped and turned. "What gives, Jess, is that I am going to send this pump to the state lab for a little work. If it reveals what I think it will, then I will finally have enough to get started on and not much more."

"Tell me, Bill. Tell me what you are thinking. What do you think you have found?"

"No, Jess. This has gone far enough. You are not to involve yourself in this matter any further. Period. If you do, I will arrest you for breaking and entering and withholding evidence. Do we understand one another?"

Jess met his stare. "I'm making no promises, Bill."

Page's voice became less hard and his body perceptibly relaxed somewhat. It was almost a shrug of resignation. "Jess, I figured out why you are doing this and it's no good, my friend. It won't help you like you think it will and just as importantly, it won't help Gary Lother. And it sure can't help Sacco."

"I'm in this thing, Bill. I've been in it since **you** said Gary died by accidental drowning."

The Sheriff saw there was no point in any further conversation. "Come on. It's getting late. Sacco will be wondering about you. Let me drop you off."

By the time they arrived at the Stevens' house, Jess managed to get the Sheriff to tell him about the sticker on the bottom of the vacuum pump that read "Inland Empire Chemical Supply Company."

CHAPTER THIRTEEN

Bill Page sat at his office desk in the Stevens County Court-house in Colville the next morning even earlier than usual. And that was early. He wanted a fast start on the day and a chance to play a little catch up on the matter of Gary Lother's death, which he no longer thought of strictly in terms of an accident.

His first call was to the State Patrol's Crime Laboratory Division in Olympia.

"This is Captain Fisher. May I help you?"

"Dave? Bill Page. How are ya'?"

"Bill! Long time no hear!" The two men had gone through the State Patrol Academy in Shelton together and were assigned to the same area as rookie troopers. Their friendship ran deep even though they did not see each other that often since Page had left the Patrol to become Sheriff. But Captain Fisher believed in his heart that he would always owe a big debt to Page, maybe even owe him his career. During their second month on the road, they were the first officers at the scene of a head-on collision that killed all the members of two families including three small children. Dave Fisher had never seen death, at least not that violent and messy, while Page had seen plenty of it in Vietnam as a medical corpsman. Page helped his young friend through the horror of that experience for weeks afterwards and Fisher never forgot it.

Their friendship was why the Sheriff called Olympia rather than go through the satellite office in Spokane. Straight-laced as he was, Page was not above pulling a string or two if it mattered. And this time, he thought it mattered.

"Still working, Dave? I'd a thought you'd hang it up as soon as you had your years in. Having too much fun?"

"Compared to the road, Bill, this is easy. Hell I may go 'till I'm forced out."

"Good. Cause I might need your help from time to time. Like now."

"Sure, Bill. What's up?"

"I've got a small vacuum pump found at the site of an arson fire. It was in the home of a boy who died last month under circumstances which may now come into question. I'm afraid the trail is going to get cold if I don't get moving fast. So, Dave, can I send this over for analysis done on the fast track?"

"No problem. You get it to me today and I will have something for you in a couple of days. Soon enough for you?"

"That'll be just fine, Dave. I appreciate it and I owe you one."

"I'm glad you feel that way because next year I'm going to hold you to your promise to take me deep sea fishing out at Westport. But I hope it won't be that long before I see you."

The men signed off with well meaning promises to see one another soon.

The Sheriff's next call was to the Drug Enforcement Authority in Spokane. It was also headed by another old friend of the Sheriff, Ron Mathison. Washington State has several million people in it yet many of the people in law enforcement seemed to know one another no matter what jurisdiction they worked in. In this case, Mathison had started in the State Patrol and had served as Page's shift supervisor during one of his assignments. Later, Mathison had taken an early retirement and gone into Federal service.

"Ron? Bill Page. How ya' doing?"

"Fine, Bill. Just sticking my fingers in the dike every day. Didn't know I had so many fingers."

"Has one of those fingers ever stuck in Inland Empire Chemical Supply Company in town down there?"

"No. Not really. We've watched 'em like we've watched all the supply houses but we've never had an issue. Matter of fact, now that I think about it, we kept a real close eye on it a few years ago when the original owner's kid, Tim something-or-other, took over for his father. That's the kind of situation where you have to watch. Nothing there that we're aware of though. Why?"

"Probably nothing, Ron. Just doing a little checking. You've talked to the Spokane Task Force people recently and your perspective is current?"

"Well, sure. We talk to them every day and I can't imagine there would be anything going on if we didn't know about it, anything at all. I can check on it to make sure and get back to you if there is."

"I'd appreciate that, Ron. While I have you on the line, is there anything going on up this way that I should know about?"

Mathison didn't say anything. After several seconds, Page asked, "Ron? Are you there?"

"Uh, yeah, Bill." He paused slightly. "We don't have anything specific or concrete in your neck of the woods at all."

Mathison was talking in code and Page picked up on it immediately.

"So, you cannot confirm anything **big** going on up here at the present time. Is that correct?"

"That is correct, Bill. If we had anything concrete we would be notifying you, of course."

This tiny fiction enabled Mathison to respect departmental procedures while still doing the right thing by someone he liked and trusted. Page would simply have to exercise some resourcefulness to take it from here. The DEA agent had no doubt about Page's ability to do that.

"Thanks, Ron. I appreciate your time."

"Sure, Bill. And if I hear anything I will be in touch. You do the same, okay?"

The Sheriff hung up and pondered what he had heard. Clearly, Mathison was telling him the DEA had suspicions about some activity in his county but wasn't ready or able to share it with him. Page pulled out a piece of paper and wrote down "Gary Lother" and then drew crude pictures of a house burning, a reflux condenser and a vacuum pump. He was no artist but had adopted this doodling technique years ago to help him think through a situation. In the past, it had proved amazingly successful.

He sat and stared at the piece of paper for nearly a half hour. Then he rose, told his aging secretary where he would be and when he would be back, got in his car and drove to the Inland Empire Chemical Supply Company in Spokane.

*   *   *

The Sheriff's problem was a lack of starting places. He was forced to follow the meager trail that led to the chemical supply company notwithstanding Mathison's report because, for the time being, he had nothing else. It was the "kick over enough rocks and eventually something will crawl out" theory. Few people realized just how much investigative work was sheer stubbornness of pursuit, however slim the prospect of material benefit. And at least in this case, it also satisfied the Sheriff's need to be thorough to a fault.

Page was met at the counter by the plump Tim, whom he recognized from his name tag as the probable second-generation owner from Mathison's comment. Perhaps it was the uniform but there was something a little more alert in Tim's manner.

"Yes?" Still monosyllabic, however, and without movement in the facial muscles.

"I'm Bill Page from Stevens County and I'd like to ask you a few questions." The Sheriff never introduced himself by title because he thought it sounded pretentious. The authority inherent in his bearing and uniform was more than sufficient to command attention.

"Go on."

"Do you sell reflux condensers and vacuum pumps?"

"Yes."

"What kind of business do you do in these two items? For example, how many of each might you sell in a month?"

"Hard to say. We don't have a sophisticated inventory control system. I'd say we do a dozen or two in a year. Both items."

"Have you sold either to this boy in the last few months?" He handed a copy of Gary Lother's last high school annual picture to Tim who took and studied it for an appropriate amount of time.

"I don't remember ever seeing him. But then, I don't know if I would. Lot of people come through that door in a month."

"How many people work the counter besides you?"

"None, really. Maybe an occasional relief if I go out to

lunch but I usually don't. The other people who work here work in back mixing the chemicals, warehousing or delivering."

"How long do you keep invoice copies?"

"If you mean do we have them for the last several months, the answer is yes."

"May I take a look at them, please?"

"Uh, yes, I suppose. But aren't you a little out of your jurisdiction here, Sheriff? I mean I want to cooperate and all but this is Spokane County, not Stevens County."

"You're right. It involves a matter in Stevens County and if you need, I can get the Spokane authorities involved. Is that your preference?"

"Look, I said you were welcome to review the invoices. I just wondered about your being from Stevens County is all. I had another fellow in here the other day asking some questions about a reflux condenser and it's just getting a little curious. What's going on?"

"Nothing yet. I'm just doing some preliminary investigation."

Tim turned his body to the filing cabinets and half pointed. "There they are. Let me know if you have any questions."

"I appreciate your cooperation but for now, I'll take a rain check on reviewing the records. I may be in touch with you later, however. Thanks again." The Sheriff didn't really want to spend the hours necessary going through months of invoices but he did want to see if Tim would allow it. Satisfied that he would, the Sheriff left, but all the way home to Colville he tried to think of what rock he could turn over next. Unfortunately, Tim had been forthcoming enough that Page concluded he hit the same dead end as Jess did and as Mathison had suggested.

*   *   *

The Sheriff had not even turned north on Division before Tim yelled for someone to watch the counter for him. As his relief arrived, he walked into the adjacent warehouse and took the steps to the upstairs office two at a time. Inside, he checked a telephone number and dialed the phone.

After several rings, a voice answered, "Hello."

"Hello, Tommy?"

"Who's asking?"

"This is Tim at Inland Empire."

"What's the matter?" Tommy's voice suddenly was filled with urgency.

"I just thought you might like to know that the Stevens County Sheriff was here a few minutes ago asking questions about reflux condensers and a vacuum pump. And showing pictures of some teenage kid. Sound familiar?"

"Yeah? What are you getting at?" Tommy sounded irritable.

"Nothing. Just thought you'd like to know. Remember, Tommy: everything I've ever sold you is legal. And I don't know what you use it for because that's your business. But it gets to be my business when people start poking around, especially the law. And by the way, there was another guy here earlier this week asking about reflux condensers, too. He said something about a boy up there as well. Lot of activity, Tommy. Thought you ought to know. That's all."

He hung up without saying good-bye or waiting for an answer or acknowledgment. On his end, Tommy stared into the phone. He slammed it down and started pacing back and forth. "Shit," he yelled and reached over and threw a kitchen chair down on the floor. It made a loud noise as it skidded into the wall.

He hurried to the cupboard where he retrieved his cup and saucer, poured himself some coffee and nervously stirred in the "Coffeemate." After a few sips, he picked the phone back up and dialed. Tommy knew what to do. He was doing the only thing he could. He was calling Big Brother.

But he had to hurry. He had a flight to catch.

CHAPTER FOURTEEN

Tommy hung up the phone from talking to Big Brother and checked himself in the hallway mirror. Today's "costume" was the Field Surveyor – chino pants, serviceable work boots, a flannel shirt, an outdoor sweater, and heavy parka.

He grabbed the familiar suitcase and carry-on and headed for the Spokane airport for the shuttle Horizon flight to Seattle. Alaska flight #395 to Fairbanks left Seattle in a little more than two hours. There was no time to spare.

Tommy hated the periodic trips to Fairbanks. He hated the hard work because if things went as usual, he would be up all night. And he especially hated dealing with John Baird. The man was big and ugly and mean and Tommy didn't trust him. Big Brother said not to worry, he knew Baird from way back. Besides, there was too much in it for Baird to spoil the deal. But Baird was loud and Tommy just knew someone would overhear them some day and get them all into trouble, big trouble.

Baird was so menacing. At six foot four, he towered over Tommy and weighed close to 300 pounds. In the middle of discussions, he would get up and glare down at Tommy, standing there with his long-flowing black beard and unkempt hair, wearing his denims, suspenders, dirty shirt and boots. The boots were huge mountainous soiled stumps of leather.

Tommy hated Fairbanks and he hated Baird but fortunately, Big Brother told him on the phone that he might not have to make this trip again, ever. Tommy couldn't tell if Big Brother was just saying that to calm him down or if he really meant it.

For a change, the airlines were running on time and Tommy landed in Fairbanks promptly at 5:59 PM. It was a quick taxi ride to the hotel where Tommy rented a suite. He needed the extra space to lay out some of the equipment and for the added degree of privacy. But just as in Los Angeles, he used a fake name, paid with cash and rotated hotels. He only wished Fairbanks had more hotels.

He took dinner in his room and was barely finished when the inevitable loud knock came. Cracking the door slightly, he looked up to see John Baird glowering in at him.

"Well, damnit, man, open the goddamn door," he thundered.

Tommy undid the safety latch and let Baird through. He carried in two metal suitcases that he handled as though they were feathers but Tommy knew each weighed many pounds.

There were no pleasantries exchanged as Baird set the suitcases on top of the table in the sitting room. He opened each up to reveal several full cloth bags. Tommy picked up a particularly lumpy one and poured the contents onto the table top. The gold nuggets clattered loudly as they hit the hard surface.

"I thought you'd like that one," the big man offered. "Prettiest goddamn bunch of nuggets I've shown you yet." Tommy thought the man never spoke a single sentence without the word "goddamn" in it. "Mind if I turn your goddamn boob tube on while you do the preliminaries?" He opened the console and started channel surfing before Tommy had a chance to answer.

Tommy took a small scale out of his suitcase and set it up on the table. He separately weighed and recorded each bag's contents on a sheet of paper. The bags were already tagged with a code on it and Tommy used the same code for his records. He also tested a sample of gold from each bag. Some he just eyeballed; he had an excellent eye for it. With others, he pressed his fingernail in to gauge the metal's softness. The softer, the better. The harder gold contained higher percentages of other ores such as copper or lead, and was less valuable. On other samples, he conducted a quick acid test. In each instance, he was attempting to get only a ballpark estimate of the purity of the gold. But while it was only an estimate, it helped him in his negotiations with Baird.

The nuggets would command the highest prices because of their special value in the market place, especially for use in jewelry. Some would be extraordinarily valuable and would lead to individual nugget by nugget bargaining. This was particularly true with the rare nugget still attached or suspended in quartz crystal. But most of the bags contained flakes, the customary product of placer's gold. These were always negotiated a whole bag at a time.

It made Tommy nervous that Baird would allow him to weigh and examine so much gold and never even cast a glance in his direction. The big man would just sit and flip through the television channels, pausing long enough on occasion to laugh uproariously. Tommy once asked him why he didn't check to make sure that everything was being recorded accurately and no stray nuggets were accidentally finding their way into Tommy's pocket. "If you did that," Baird bellowed, "I'd have to pull out my gun and blow your goddamn sorry ass away." From then on, Tommy lived in abject fear that Baird would accuse him of stealing, even though he hadn't, and kill him anyway.

Eventually, the bargaining began. The bags of flakes went fairly quickly. But one bag of nuggets took nearly an hour and things seemed to slow down. Tommy hated the give and take with Baird who was clearly trying to gain ridiculous advantage. "Look, you little shit," Baird yelled, "I have twenty miners out in the Yukon who work their goddamn asses off every goddamn day for this stuff. Don't you be low balling me like this. I might make you go out in the fields and deal with them mean sonabitches. If you think I'm gruff, you lil' pencil dick, them goddamn assholes drink piss from a dirty boot every day."

This was a variation on the same speech Baird gave every time they met. Tommy tried to remain calm but he was certain the big man would explode in violence at some perceived insult one day. He devoutly hoped this would be his last meeting. As evenly as he could, he would respond that Baird and the men were getting top dollar. "In fact, John, they – and you – are getting a substantial premium. We've consistently paid you at least twenty percent above the market. Probably twenty-five percent, truth be known."

"Yeah, and it's worth it to you or you wouldn't do it. So don't give me that goddamn line."

It **was** worth it to Tommy and Big Brother. Baird didn't know why although he could guess. For the time being he would push it as far as he could and no further. After all, he **had** made several hundred thousand dollars off these dealings in the last year. And the miners he represented still came out far ahead of where they could with the usual commercial buyers. Besides the premium price they were paid, dealing "privately" like this enabled the miners to hide a lot the money and avoid taxes.

Back and forth it went all night long. Occasionally the men would just stop talking and rest or go to the bathroom. Once, Tommy snuck a little "Coffeemate" while in the bathroom. It was the last of his supply and he wanted to save it, but the big man was getting on his nerves. He would just take his chances that he would be all right for a few days.

For a while, progress was steady but discussions eventually bogged down again. Finally, it came down to the last bag, the one Tommy had first opened, the one with the large nuggets. The haggling took two hours as they went nugget by nugget. Mostly Baird would try to intimidate and mostly, he succeeded. Tommy tried to stay calm on the exterior even though he was scared to death on the inside. When they were almost through, Tommy stopped to calculate his total purchases. They were getting close to consuming all the cash he brought.

"Okay. Okay. Okay. It's a deal. We're done," Tommy finally said with exasperation, agreeing to pay a higher price for the last few nuggets than he should have. But he no longer cared. He just wanted it over. It was nearly six AM and he was exhausted from lack of sleep and from the constant intimidation. He told Big Brother many times he didn't want to do this but Big Brother insisted, claiming he had to maintain the fiction of his day-time job. "Besides," he told Tommy, "you know more about the metal than I do. I'll go up a couple of times with you when I can. You'll do fine."

Tommy counted out the cash while Baird turned television back on. He was tempted to tell the big man good-bye for good and tell him off, tell him what a son of a bitch he thought he was. Something in him, something instinctively cautious or afraid, told him to hold back. It probably saved his life. Baird would not have hesitated to cut Tommy's throat right in the hotel room and take both the cash and the gold if he knew Tommy would not keep coming back and making the purchases that were making Baird a rich man.

Tommy transferred the cash to Baird's two smaller metal suitcases and placed all the cloth bags in his larger suitcase. It made it very heavy but he was pleased with the night's work. He had just enough cash to get to Seattle, take care of his business and get home. And with any luck, he would never have to do this again.

After a long shower and a big breakfast, Tommy checked out of the hotel and took a taxi to the Fairbanks airport where he caught the eight-thirty AM flight to Seattle. He slept almost the entire five hours of the trip. The flight attendant tried but couldn't wake him for lunch.

Tommy took a taxi straight from SeaTac airport to the plant in the Georgetown section of south Seattle. It was a relatively short drive on Interstate Five and off at the Albro exit that didn't require him to risk much in the way of the ever-increasing Seattle traffic. Usually, traffic congealed on the interstate north of Albro, next to the former Rainier Brewery. With the slightest provocation, however, the whole freeway could become a mess from downtown south for miles, even past Boeing air field. Seattle's traffic had become a serious problem and not just in terms of efficiency or convenience. The congestion was a blight on the beautiful community's self-identity, an identity of enormous pride. It was an ugly, environmental cancer in the nation's self-proclaimed environmental capital, and an irritating reminder of the area's impotence to solve its own problems.

A tall, thin patrician man, who was older than he looked, greeted Tommy as the taxi pulled up to the business office in front of the Trevison Metal Refinery. Proud and dignified, he had the easy assurance of a successful man who had a few of life's mysteries figured out. He moved deliberately and was kind to everyone – quite a contrast to his younger years when he was building the business. Then, he made a name for himself by his rough and tumble purchases among miners throughout the world. In several mining magazines, he ran an advertisement showing himself hanging from a helicopter by one hand with a briefcase in the other. **"No Place We Won't Go"** the headline screamed.

And it was true. Roger Trevison delighted in pursuing the independent miners on their turf, cash in hand. He relished the game of bargaining with them and even the occasional fist fights such efforts inevitably yielded. But he mellowed with age and he no longer missed the field work. Now, he was content with the easy and automatic flow of business established over time. And he genuinely enjoyed the unhurried company of his customers – even the newer ones like Tommy who had become an important part of Trevison Metal Refinery.

"Do you want to watch them do the testing, Tommy, or do you want to go down to my office and put your feet up? Your choice, son." Trevison liked Tommy, whom he considered to be an irritable and troubled soul, but one with a good heart. Tommy was about the age of his two sons, both of whom worked at the plant, and Trevison felt a little fatherly toward him. Tommy responded to the feeling. Somehow, around Trevison, he was less nervous than usual.

"Tommy," he said as they sat down in his office, "you know I never want to intrude or interfere in another man's business?"

"Yes, Mr. Trevison, I do." Tommy always called him Mr. Trevison, out of respect, and the older man had given up trying to get him to call him Roger.

"Well, I hope you will take this in the spirit in which it is intended but do you think it's safe to be traveling with that much product?" He always called gold "product." "There is a lot of value there, son, and there is some risk."

"I'm fine, sir. I take certain precautions," Tommy answered.

"Good. Glad to hear it." Trevison let it drop. He learned long ago in business relationships not to ask questions unless invited to do so. He never violated this rule with Tommy because he didn't want to upset him; he sensed his fragility. And besides liking Tommy, he was a damned important customer. So much so that he never broached the subject of the source of gold. He tried a couple of times in very oblique terms and Tommy simply referenced the "family's several claims." But that is as far as it went. "What the hell," Trevison thought, "the federal government doesn't require me to record the source of this stuff – and it requires me to record every other conceivable activity – why should I care?" And he didn't.

After a couple of hours, the lab report was done on the bags of gold. Tommy and Trevison began the process of price settlement. These weren't negotiations so much as they were discussions. Trevison was always fair and thorough. Tommy trusted him as much as he could trust anyone and so, it was little work on Tommy's part. Today, he was pleased because the price of gold had begun to move up recently. Industrial consumption was on the steady rise as new applications for the metal and its special properties were discovered. Trevison was doing a great business. His small research team had made great progress on improving the purification process and as a result, he was signing new contracts for customers all over the world in photographic equipment and computers as well as jewelry.

Still, when all was said and done, Tommy and Big Brother took a big hit on the double transaction. Big Brother said it didn't matter. They were making so much money that "legitimizing" it was just another cost of doing business. Tommy wondered if there was any way they could ever legitimize this money.

"Huh? What?" Tommy asked, snapping out of his trance.

"I was just asking you, Tommy, if you wanted a check for the gold or if you wanted it deposited in your account."

"Put it in the account, please, Mr. Trevison."

"You know, Tommy, you're getting to have quite a bit in your account. Of course, we're glad to manage this for you but the truth is, we didn't establish this service for amounts like this."

He handed Tommy a statement of his balance. Tommy stared down at the piece of paper trying to comprehend what the many millions of dollars actually meant.

"We invest very conservatively as a temporary convenience to our suppliers but frankly, I think you should consider moving your money to a business that is designed to handle this sum of money."

Tommy didn't know it but at that very moment, plans were being made to move the money out of the Trevison account – and soon.

CHAPTER FIFTEEN

Just as Tommy's plane was landing at SeaTac International Airport earlier that morning, Sheriff Page was sitting in his office in Colville doodling on a piece of paper. They were the same doodles he drew earlier in the week and they provided no new inspiration and suggested no new rocks to kick over. For now, all he could do was wait for the report back from the state crime lab. So he doodled and waited all day long.

Hours later, his reverie was finally broken by an incoming call in mid-afternoon. His elderly and overly protective assistant was down the hall, and so he grabbed the phone himself, hoping it was Dave Fisher at the crime lab. It wasn't.

"This is Bill Page."

"Sheriff? Sheriff Page?"

"Yes. Who is this, please?"

"My name's Ashby, Dick Ashby. I live up here on Chewelah Golf Course. Retired up here a couple of years ago from California. Best move of my life."

Chewelah was becoming a popular destination for retirees, especially those from California who could sell their homes for a small fortune, replace them in Chewelah, and live on the interest from the profits they made. The mini-wave of in-migration was started by an article in a popular national senior citizens' publication featuring the virtues of Chewelah with its small town atmosphere, natural beauty and low cost of living. The older population earned the community its nickname as "St. Peter's Waiting Room."

"How can I help you, Mr. Ashby?"

"I was out in the woods this morning. Pretty early, about seven or so. And anyway, I saw something and I don't know what it is but I thought you ought to know about it."

The Sheriff found himself glad to get the call, glad to get his mind off the Lother situation. Besides, important leads often came into his office in just this way, a telephone call from a conscientious citizen.

"Please, just describe exactly what you saw and where you saw it."

"I was in the woods, like I said. Next month is hunting season, you know, and I like to get out and hike around a little the month before. Get in better shape than just golfing will do for ya' although I always walk. Can't stand those electric carts one bit." Page was beginning to reevaluate how happy he was to receive this call. "Anyway, it never hurts to get out and get a feel for what the deer are doing either. But the main thing is I don't want to drop dead of a heart attack in the middle of the woods. That happened to a friend of mine a few years ago. It was awful. Damn glad I wasn't with him at the time, you know?"

"Mr. Ashby," the Sheriff interrupted, "can you tell me where you were?"

"Oh, yeah, sure. I was east of Chewelah off the Flowery Trail Road – you know the one." Page did know it. He knew the entire county but he loved the Chewelah area. He invented every excuse possible to spend time in

Chewelah just so he could eat at his favorite restaurant, Polanski's Pizza, on the edge of town. "Anyway, I drove up the Flowery Trail Road about a mile past McPherson Spring on the way to that ski resort – what do they call it?"

"49 Degrees North," the Sheriff offered. The small ski resort had had its business ups and downs but in a county as depressed as Stevens, it was a real boost to the economy in the dead of winter.

"Right. Right. That's the one. Not a skier myself, never cared for the sport. Always thought the lift tickets were highway robbery. Anyway, about a mile past McPherson Spring, I turned left on an unmarked road and followed it another mile or so until it dead-ended. Then I hiked up another mile or so when I came across it."

"What is 'it', Mr. Ashby?"

"Well, I'm not sure but if I didn't know any better, I'd say it was the remnants of a small lab of some sort. There was a small lean-to kind of a set-up with a portable table and a little generator and a bunch of glassware and the like. The lean-to was back in the trees a bit and hidden. I only saw it by accident. The open side was turned into the hillside and the back was sort of camouflaged. Anyway, it was fairly fresh although there wasn't any sign someone had been there in the last few days."

"You didn't touch anything, did you?" The Sheriff wasn't so much concerned with disturbing evidence as he was with the potential for toxic danger. He immediately decided he needed to take a look at this himself and see if it would be necessary to bring some clean-up experts in. If it was an abandoned drug lab, it could be a lethal hazard to some unsuspecting or curious hunter or hiker. Page would then call the DEA or the State Patrol's narcotics section and they would get the state Department of Ecology's hazardous spill response team involved. It would be a big hassle but a necessary precaution.

"No, sir. I didn't."

"Good. Would you have time to show me exactly where you saw this? Say, in about an hour?"

"Well, yeah. I guess. I was supposed to go do the shopping with the Mrs. but I think she will understand. Tell you what, I'll meet you right where I parked my car. Right there at the end of that road off Flowery Trail, the one about a mile past McPherson Spring. An hour would be fine. Sure."

The Sheriff hung up the phone with slight trepidation about all the listening he had in store later. He slid a piece of blank paper across his desk and drew a picture of a lean-to along with new sketches of a reflux condenser, vacuum pump and burning house. He connected the four objects with lines so that he had a square shape with an "x" in it. Underneath, he wrote, "Connected?"

After thirty minutes of staring at the paper and not receiving a call from Dave Fisher, he got up, put his jacket on and told his assistant he probably wouldn't be back until the morning but to leave a message on his home machine if Captain Fisher called back. On his way out, he muttered under his breath, "Sometimes, maybe the rocks come to you."

*   *   *

Page pulled his Sheriff's car to a slow stop at the end of the dirt road. The mixed Ponderosa pines and Douglas firs towered around him. A large bar gate blocked further access ahead where the timber awaited its next harvesting in another twenty or thirty years.

In front of the gate was a grassy area just large enough to turn his car around in. Instinctively, he did so, pointing the car back out should he need to leave quickly. Before leaving his office, he considered bringing the department's four-wheel drive vehicle but decided against it. The dirt road was fairly primitive and remote but still dry from the long summer.

Sitting at his desk inside all day had stiffened his muscles and clouded his brain. He left the car radio on and got out to stretch and breathe in the fresh, pine-scented woods air. September was his favorite month and this day was proving why. Pleasant days and cool but not chilly evenings. There was a certain quiet in the air, maybe the pause before the change of season when the nights would grow cold and the deciduous trees would explode with red and yellow color.

The Sheriff took another deep breath, held it for a moment before slowly exhaling and leaning back against his car, letting the sun strike him full in the face. It was warm and felt good. Out of the corner of his eye he kept watch for his guide to the suspected lab.

The Sheriff wasn't a religious man but he gave brief thanks for the uncompromising beauty of the land he called home and the community in which he had a friend in every town. "So much better than the road," he thought. He was glad those days were gone. He could think of no where on earth he would rather live.

At that moment, he "saw" a bright light, not with his eyes but with his mind. It was a brilliant, instant burst that flashed sudden images. He saw a wedding picture from his youth in which he stood straight and tanned in a naval uniform. His young bride was beautiful and radiant, smiling a smile from deep inside her. And he saw an image of Gary Lother's body being loaded into an ambulance for its last journey to the medical examiner's office in Spokane. Bill Page had no idea why he saw these two particular images and his brain had no time to ponder the question. His brain had been shredded by the bullet of a high-powered rifle on the ridge above him.

Death was not instantaneous but close to it. Life left him with the same swift movement as air enters a vacuum. There was no chance for last regrets or last utterances or last anything. No chance to react and no chance to know who the enemy was.

His assassin rose from his prone position on the ridge 200 yards away. It was a good, clean shot, he thought. The body immediately went limp and fell lifeless to the ground. It reminded him of the first time he saw a steer shot in the field for slaughter. He wondered back then if a human body would respond the same way. Now he knew.

He shouldered the bolt-action 30.06 Winchester hunting rifle with its powerful Leupold variable scope and quickly looked around on the ground for any sign he might leave behind. He wasn't too worried, though. This was the perfect spot for an assassination. There weren't any homes for miles around and the sound wasn't likely to be heard. The Sheriff's body could lie there for days before anyone found him. And when they did find the body, it would take them a while to figure out where the shot came from and to retrace his probable path. By then, he would be long gone and they would never find him. Big Brother was pleased and let out a small involuntary giggle.

He turned and briskly walked down the backside of the mountain in the direction of his vehicle, parked a mile away. As he left, he didn't hear the sound of the motorcycle starting up two ridges over. The motorcyclist had stopped to rest and drink from his canteen before heading home for dinner. He heard the rifle shot and thought it was curious at least, ominous at worst. Hunting season was several weeks away, a time when he would never enter this area. Too many crazy hunters.

He took the long way home in the direction of the

rifle shot. Minutes later Sheriff Page's body was discovered long before the assassin planned.

*   *   *

Two hours later, Jess and Sacco were sitting on their deck enjoying a quiet, pleasant meal. It was the leftover lasagna from Sheriff Page's visit two days earlier. Jess thought re-heated lasagna had an even fuller flavor than fresh-baked lasagna. He could easily eat these leftovers two or three times a week without complaint.

"How was your day, paisan?" he asked.

"Same-o, same-o. Two students suspended. One student expelled. One crying teacher whose wife told him she was leaving him and he could keep the kids. I'm not sure what upset him more. Two dozen wonderful, crazy teenagers who presented me with a cake at lunch just because. And one angry union representative."

"What's the union story?"

"A grievance. Seems my vice principal evaluated a teacher in the building and didn't follow the rules in the collective bargaining agreement."

"A good teacher?"

"Very good, as a matter of fact. It was all just a misunderstanding but things got out of hand."

"What are you going to do?" Jess loved to hear these stories of daily life in the world of Sacco's high school. He also loved to hear how she managed these matters because she was so good at her job and he marveled at her ability. In fact, he was proud of her. But before she could answer, the phone rang. Both rose to get it but Jess waved her down. "Finish eating," he mumbled through a mouthful of food.

A few minutes later, Jess returned to the deck and sat down, staring blankly out at the lake.

"Who was that, Gumbah?" Sacco asked absently as

she continued to chew her bread.

"Ben," Jess answered.

"What's on his mind? Besides fishing?"

"Sacco," he said evenly, "I have some bad news."

She looked up at him and noticed that he was pale. "Jess," she said with concern, "are you all right?"

"It's Bill Page, paisan. He's been murdered."

"Oh, my God," she blurted, dropping her napkin onto her unfinished plate of food. "Oh, my God," she repeated. "What happened?"

"They're not sure, according to Ben. Evidently, some motorcyclist was riding up in the woods east of Chewelah and found his body. He was . . . he was shot through the head."

Sacco buried her face in her hands. She didn't cry or seem to breathe at all for several minutes but Jess could feel her agony. Finally, she inhaled deeply and looked up. "Do they have any idea who or why?"

"No, nothing. The biker just heard a shot and went looking and found Bill lying next to his car up off the Flowery Trail Road and then let the Sheriff's office in Colville know. It just happened a couple of hours ago but you know what they say about bad news traveling around the world in the time it takes good news to get up and put its shoes on in the morning. I imagine everyone in eastern Washington will know before it hits the eleven o'clock news."

"It's just so . . . so senseless and wasted. He was such a good man."

"Very good. And very professional. And it got him killed," he added.

Sacco looked up with a slightly puzzled expression. "What do you mean? I thought you said they had nothing, no idea what happened."

"**They** may have nothing. But I think I know who killed him. Or at least why."

"What are you talking about, Gumbah? What exactly are you saying?"

"I'm saying Bill was killed by the same person or the same people who killed Gary Lother. Actually, now that I think about it, it's obvious." The color had returned to his face and his whole body was beginning to tighten and intensify. Sacco recognized the sign and didn't like it.

"So?" she asked.

"So, you're right. It was senseless and wasted."

Sacco waited but nothing came. She bit her lip in a failed attempt to give herself something else to think about, a distracting pain. She didn't want to say anything now, to ask Jess about what was on her mind for fear that it would suggest something to him that he had not thought of himself. But she realized it was futile as the look of determination crept into his eyes and grew. It was part determination and part rage but it was the determination that worried her most.

"You're not planning on doing anything about it . . . are you?" she finally asked quietly.

"Well, yes. As a matter of fact, I am."

"Jess, I don't know if that is wise."

"We've been through this already, Sacco."

"No, Jess, we haven't. We were 'through this' before Bill was murdered. And if his death did have something to do with Gary Lother's death, then we haven't been through this at all."

"I can help."

"No, Jess. You're not helping. You're trying to solve another problem and we both know it. Jess. Gumbah. Darling." She came around the table and kneeled on the deck next to him taking his forearm in her hands. "Nothing can take away that pain. Nothing except maybe time. But certainly not this."

For an instance, she thought she saw a flicker of pain in his eyes, a slight clouding of the determination and she thought it might be possible to reach him.

"I think you're also feeling responsible for this in some way because you suspected the Lother boy didn't drown and you think this is all tied in. Well, it may be and it may not be. We don't know. But you're sitting there thinking if you hadn't said anything to Bill about your suspicions, he might be alive tonight. You simply can't take responsibility for everything. You just can't do it."

"You're right. On all counts." He said it very calmly.

"Jess, listen to me." He looked into her eyes. "The last year has been the worst year of our lives. And God willing, we won't ever have to go through anything that painful again. But this won't help. I am asking you to please, please, stop this now!" It was her last card to play, to plead. In twenty years she had never begged him for anything.

He said nothing and she realized it was too late. He had become unreachable.

She put her head down on his arm and gently stroked his fingers and worried about the man she loved with all her heart. "What are you going to do?" she asked with quiet resignation.

"For starters, I am going back down to Inland Empire Chemical Supply. I know Bill went down there yesterday. Maybe he saw something that led to this."

One last idea occurred to her. "Why don't you at least call some authorities? Call the chief of the State Patrol. After all, he's a friend of yours."

Jess looked down at her with a sudden and surprised awareness and snapped his fingers. "That's a great idea, paisan." He jumped up, almost knocking her to the deck, and ran into the house leaving Sacco sitting.

Once inside, he called the number of the security shack outside the Governor's mansion in Olympia. The State patrol provided twenty-four hour coverage to the mansion with the services of cadets from the State Patrol Academy in nearby Shelton. It was a part of their training.

"May I speak to the Governor, please," Jess asked. "This is Jess Stevens."

"Yes, sir. Just a moment, sir," the cadet said politely, instantly recognizing the name.

After a moment, the deep, familiar voice came on the line. "Jesse, what a pleasant surprise. Great to hear from you. I was just about to give **you** a call. What's up?"

"Governor, I have some bad news. Sheriff Bill Page of Stevens County was murdered late this afternoon by an unknown assailant. It just happened a couple of hours ago."

Jess heard the Governor sigh loudly. "I'm sorry to hear that, Jesse. I didn't know him well but he seemed like a real professional and a decent person. I always listened when Bill spoke. Did he have any family?"

"No, sir. He has – had – an ex-wife. They were divorced a few years ago but there were no children."

"I appreciate your letting me know, Jesse. I assume the State Patrol has been contacted already? Seems to me I remember that Bill was in the Patrol for a few years."

"I presume they have. I think everyone in this part of the state already knows. But, Governor, uh, this isn't a strictly FYI call. I'm looking for some help."

"What's on your mind?"

"Two things, actually, Governor. The first is easy, easier than the second but I need them both." Jess explained his requests to the Governor who listened without interrupting until Jess was finished.

"This seems a little out of your line, to say the least, isn't it, Jesse?" the Governor asked.

"Yes, sir." Jess responded but added nothing in the way of defense or explanation. He could almost hear the

Governor's wheels turning on the other end of the line. The state's top politician was known for taking risks but they were bold, few, far between and calculated. This request had some liabilities and didn't seem to fit in.

"Jesse, I told you when you left this town I would do anything I could for you. But I never imagined it would be something like this."

Jess knew he had him. As soon as the Governor reminded himself of his words to Jess last winter, he would get there. He was good for his word. And Jess and he had been close, much closer than any two people who had ever occupied their respective positions. In the state capital, conventional wisdom was that the Governor and the Speaker, even when members of the same political party, would end up as competitors sooner or later, just as a matter of institutional friction. Not so with Jess and the Governor. They genuinely liked and respected one another. They were a rare exception to the norm – their personal friendship transcended their own political self-interest.

"Okay, Jesse. Okay," he finally said. "Please just watch out for yourself. Will tomorrow afternoon be okay?"

"That'll be fine, Governor. Thank you." This time he hung up without waiting for further words from the Governor. He was in a hurry. He was going back down to Trent Street in Spokane, to the Inland Empire Chemical Supply Company.

CHAPTER SIXTEEN

It was after nine o'clock by the time Jess left the lake for Spokane. But first, he and Sacco cleaned the dishes and made busy around the house, avoiding talking to one another. Jess dressed in his used breaking-and-entering garb, but this time there was no sense of adventure or excitement, only purpose. Sacco's new resistance would not deter him but it did have a sobering effect on preparations.

As he started to leave, Sacco remained on the deck looking out at the lake. It was a moonless night with a light cloud cover, enough to obscure the normally bright stars. Even the distant lights of Spokane, usually a faint glow in the southern horizon, were not visible. The darkness made the lake feel more isolated and deserted than usual. Above and around the deck, the trees were noisy with motion; the wind was blowing hard enough to make them sway back and forth in a loud dance. Sacco stood staring in the water's direction with her arms crossed. She wore a luxurious, white chenille bathrobe, a birthday gift from Jess she thought entirely too extravagant but one she loved.

Jess quietly walked up behind her and rested his hands on her shoulders and leaned into her with his chest and hips. She placed both her hands over his and tilted her head back without saying anything. He loved her touch, her smell, the feel of her wiry hair against his face, of her body next to his. He drew comfort from the embrace and thought how much the small, strong woman meant to him and always had. He could barely remember life without her.

His will on the matter at hand was resolute and had been from the beginning. But for the first time, standing there holding her, he wondered, ever so briefly. For a tiny instant, it occurred to him that someone other than himself was very much involved and very much affected.

"*Ti amo*," he whispered quickly and turned to leave, his resolve returning. Sacco stood staring at the darkness and the lake. Jess didn't see the tears on her face.

Traffic was light on the way in to Spokane on Highway 395. Few people traveled south at this time of night during the week. Sunday evenings were another matter. That was when the people from Spokane who owned cabins on Loon Lake or nearby Deer Lake would head back to town and make the highway feel like one big thirty-five mile parking lot.

All the way to Spokane, Jess listened to classical music on the car radio. It was "thinking" music for him because it seemed to stimulate his creative impulses. And right now he was trying to imagine what he might be looking for once inside the Inland Empire Chemical Supply Company.

Shortly after arriving on Trent Street and parking the car a block away from Inland Empire, Jess realized he should have spent his time thinking about how to get into the building. This wasn't the Lother house where Jess knew the location of an extra key that would open the front door.

For thirty minutes, he carefully examined the building. The front side had three access points. The main entrance door, heavy metal with multiple locks. The front display window with its chemistry kits. And a large delivery bay, closed and locked tight. There were a few windows at the top of the warehouse portion of the building but they were out of reach. The back of the building had no windows, another single impenetrable door and another delivery bay directly to the rear of the front one. All doors and windows, even the ones out of reach at the top of the building, appeared to be secured by the tape and wires of a contact security system. Forcible entry would bring the police in a matter of seconds. And Jess might need a long time in the building.

He returned to his car to think or pout, he wasn't sure which. Literally breaking in was out of the question. Even without the security system, the noise would probably bring police from neighboring Idaho. He thought about the roof for a while, wondering if there would be some inside access on top of the roof. But short of a ladder or a helicopter, he couldn't see how he could scale the height. He gave a moment's thought to trying to figure out how to disable the alarm system – but only a moment. If he was lucky enough to find some outside controls, he would probably electrocute himself.

In despair, Jess reached for the ignition to begin the trip home in defeat when suddenly, his luck changed. A semi-truck with a car right behind it pulled up in front of the building. While the driver from the car got out and opened up the bay door and the truck driver was opening the back of his truck, Jess quietly snuck out of his car and took up a position just around the corner of the building at the opposite end from the bay area. This near-midnight delivery seemed somewhat suspicious to him.

"Sorry for being so late. I've never broken down like that before and it's really good of you to come down at this ridiculous hour." It was the truck driver's voice and then Jess heard a short, muffled response but he couldn't make out the words.

"I'm double lucky," the truck driver continued as he guided his hand cart down the pull out ramp in the back of the truck. "Lucky I could get that engine part in Montana and lucky you were good enough to come down here tonight even though I'm several hours behind schedule. I might even be able to make up the time to Portland."

That sounded innocent enough to Jess but the important thing was the opportunity this presented. He realized the unloading wouldn't last indefinitely and that he needed to act quickly to exploit the situation. He couldn't just tip-toe into the warehouse. The two men were back and forth with their hand trucks too fast for him to go undetected. Instead, he needed a diversion.

His salvation sat on a pole a few yards behind him on the sidewalk. It wasn't an original idea or very clever or even legal for that matter. But it seemed straightforward and effective.

The ancient looking metal fire alarm box resembled a bird house with a glass door in front. With his light jacket wrapped several times around a handy rock, Jess waited until the two men were both in the warehouse and then shattered the glass with a muffled pop. He pulled down the small lever and quickly retreated to the side of the nearest building in anticipation of a screaming alarm. But nothing happened.

"Great," he thought. "A busted fire alarm. What can go wrong next?"

Through the stillness of the night air, he could faintly hear a ticking sound like an egg timer, coming from the box.

"Oh, so it's going to blow up, too," he whispered sarcastically. "Time for Plan B."

But before he had time to come up with or implement another plan, Jess heard the distant sound of a siren. As it grew louder and louder, he realized he had pulled the switch of a silent alarm and help was on the way.

"Back to Plan A," he said out loud, scooting around the back of the building and behind the chemical supply warehouse.

The sound of the siren was ear-splitting as the fire truck pulled up along side the alarm box on the street. When the two men in the warehouse made their way down the street to ask the firefighters about the commotion, Jess scampered inside behind their backs. Once inside, he surveyed the massive room for the best possibility of concealment and quickly chose a place beneath the stairs to the second floor office, behind two fifty gallon barrels. He made himself as small as possible and concentrated on restoring his heart rate and breathing to normal.

Minutes later, after the fire alarm had been repaired and the fire fighters were departing, the two men began unloading the rest of the truck, cursing "those damn kids" for the earlier mischief. The truck driver reiterated his gratitude to the other man, whom Jess now recognized by his portly profile as Tim, the owner, and left. Tim pressed the button to close the bay door electronically and got in his car before the door was completely shut. Jess gave passing thought to rushing out and body rolling under the door as it slowly made its way to the ground. Suddenly he was feeling trapped and alone. And a little nervous.

After waiting ten full minutes, Jess rose and pulled a tiny flashlight from his pocket. He proceeded gently, aware that the only remaining threat would be if the security system included motion or sound detectors. Using the flashlight discriminatingly, he slowly walked around looking for the tell-tale equipment that would require a hasty retreat. Satisfied that the security system was designed exclusively for unwanted entry, he moved to the interior door to the front office.

"Better to be lucky than good," he mumbled as the door opened without resistance.

Once inside, Jess immediately headed for the filing cabinets on the back wall. The three cabinets to the left were marked "sales invoices." Jess looked in the far left cabinet and found each drawer arranged by month and each month containing a carbonless copy of all invoices. The cabinet he started in was three years old, the amount of time the Internal Revenue Service requires the information to be kept. Jess found the records to be neat and orderly and for some reason, it surprised him.

He continued looking quickly in each drawer until he found the records for the last year and then began a thorough examination of each document. If need be, he could move back to the older records later but his guess was, anything worth having would be found in the last year.

While the records were neat, they were also difficult to read. The carbonless copies weren't always clear and the handwriting was often illegible. The information recorded was totally inconsistent. Sometimes, the name and address were indicated, sometimes not. Sometimes the equipment part or chemical was indicated, sometimes just the code was written down. There was no pattern save perhaps the time restraints on the recorder, presumably Tim.

The search was painfully slow and after two and a half hours, Jess was through the first eight months of records with nothing interesting to show for his efforts except severe eye strain from trying to decipher the hard to read material with too little light for the task. In addition, his head hurt from the smell of the carbonless paper. He was certain that prolonged exposure to the sharp, acidic smell of the chemically treated paper would addle his brain.

Needing a break, he walked back into the warehouse and casually deposited some change in the soft drink machine. The can made a loud noise as it dropped to the bottom for removal. Jess sat down on a nearby step, rubbing his neck with one hand and drinking the cold liquid down with the other. Soon, his optimism restored and his body refreshed by the rest and liquid nourishment, he popped up and headed back to the office for more work.

Back in the office, the very next invoice he looked at finally revealed something but not before he passed over it once without noticing. As he continued, something in the back of his mind nagged at him to return to it. All evening he had been afraid of missing something worthwhile even though it was right in front of him and he was determined not to let that happen.

Jess picked the invoice up and stared at it for several minutes, hoping that time would fully explain what was written on the paper. "What do I make of this?" he mused. He wasn't sure what to make of it. It was curious and maybe nothing more. On the other hand, maybe it was worth following up on. He just didn't know.

He did know he was getting so tired that he was sure to miss something if the search continued at the same pace and took the rest of the night. He pocketed the invoice and picked up the pace through the remaining few months' of invoices from the last year. When he finished, he had nothing new and his headache was back with a pounding vengeance.

"I surrender," he said out loud, surprising himself with the sound of his voice. "But I may return."

As calmly as he had walked out of the Lother house, he exited the back door in the warehouse and returned to his car on the street, never realizing he tripped the contact alarm when he left.

It was nearly four AM by the time Jess parked his car in the garage, entered his bedroom and pulled off his clothes. Bone weary, he carelessly let his clothes lie on the floor and softly slid under the covers trying not to wake Sacco. It was an unnecessary precaution. She turned to him without saying a word and put her arms around him, pressing her naked body close to his.

"*Ti amo*," she whispered. He smiled at her in the dark.

Tired as he was, they made love, even more passionately than usual. They communicated through this intimacy, more than they could through language, a profound sense of caring and affection. And concern.

When they were finally done, he kissed her softly on the lips and on the forehead and rolled over and fell into a deep, deep sleep. Sacco stroked the place on his right shoulder bearing his scar. It was the internal wound she thought about, however.

*   *   *

The bright light of the noon sun through the windows finally pried open his eyes. Jess wondered if his exhausted body had withstood Sacco's attempts to roust him for the morning run – he couldn't remember resisting her – or if she had just taken pity on him and let him sleep. Glancing at the clock, he was surprised at the hour.

"Hey, lazy head," he said to himself, but rather than getting up immediately, he reached over and turned the radio on softly so his body could gradually adjust to light and movement. The second phase of his leisurely morning was a shower so long he ran out of hot water in both water tanks, a small consolation for missing Sacco's company.

By the time Jess was fully dressed and in motion he

was more hungry than tired. He fired up the Bayliner for the quick run over to Granite Point to have lunch with Ben and engage in gruff repartee about nothing important. Right now he didn't want to consciously think about what he found last night or Bill Page's death or Gary Lother. It was time, he concluded, that he let his subconscious shoulder a little of the burden. Sometimes he did his best thinking when he wasn't thinking at all.

Ben refused to cooperate. He kept bringing up the murder of the popular Sheriff and babbling about the tidal wave of rumors drowning the county, no new information at all, just rumors. And one of the rumors was that a trainload of law enforcement people from the State Patrol and the FBI had descended upon Stevens County and were, at that very moment, combing through the hills around where Page's body was found as well as scouring through the dead Sheriff's files.

"It won't be long before they get the bastard," Ben offered. "Whoever he is. Cops can't afford to have someone do in one of their own and get away with it."

Jess doubted that. Whoever was behind this was smart and cunning. And careful. His guess was that there would be as little to go on as in the case of Gary Lother. But he didn't say anything. He just kept trying to change the subject and after three failed attempts, Ben got the message and reverted to his customary form of torture – where to catch them and how – all capped off by the incessant reminder of his trophy catch.

"That was inspiring, you old fart," Jess teased. "I think I'll go catch my dinner." He slid off the stool, paid his bill, and took Ben's verbal arrows in the back as he left for the boat. Three hours later, with one large kokanee in the bucket, he headed for home. It was the first time he had been fishing since he found Gary Lother's body. Those three weeks now seemed like a year to him.

Jess was more anxious than usual to see Sacco whom

he hoped would be home any minute. "She has fish to clean," he said smiling to himself.

No sooner had he entered the house and washed the fish smell from his hands than the phone rang.

"Jesse," the distinctive voice said, "I'm getting back to you on your two requests. I think I've got something here for you although I'll be damned if I know what it means."

"Let me get a pencil and pad, Governor. I want to make sure I get this down correctly."

For the next ten minutes Jess wrote down virtually everything the Governor said. He interrupted only twice to ask for clarification.

"That's it, Jesse. Pretty interesting stuff. If you want more, I can have the Chief give you a call. I told him – I **had** to tell him – the request for this information came from you. He was pretty curious about why you wanted it and what you were going to do with it. Does it help at all, Jesse?"

Jess was unable to speak. He couldn't believe it but it was right there on the piece of paper staring him in the face. How long would he have to live, he thought, before he finally and truly learned that you just never know about people. He had seen so much in his life. In war. In a career in politics. Even in the classroom. He had seen unbelievable acts of courage and reprehensible acts of greed and cowardice. He knew, he had experienced, the depths and heights of human behavior. And he had deluded himself into thinking he understood and was prepared for most anything. This stunned him, however.

"Thank you, Governor. I will call you tomorrow," he said without answering the Governor's question. And for the second time in two days, he hung up without waiting for the Governor to say "good-bye."

Jess went straight to the master bedroom upstairs and unlocked Sacco's cedar wedding chest in the corner. He dug deep. Beneath the beautiful afghan, hand knitted by Sacco's immigrant grandmother with whom he had danced the tarantella at his wedding. Beneath the miscellaneous and surplus doilies. Beneath the spare pillow cases and table cloths that were never used. Beneath a small box of military decorations. Finally, he lifted the box out and opened it.

Inside was a nine millimeter Beretta hand gun and hip holster. Jess removed the weapon from the holster and checked the action. He picked up the clip that held fifteen bullets in it and snapped it into the butt of the gun and jerked the barrel to feed one into the chamber. Taking no chances, he grabbed his extra clip and stuffed it into his pants pocket.

It was the first time the Beretta had been out of its box and holster since Jess first broke it in on the firing range. The gun was a peculiar but special gift to him from the members of the State Patrol's Executive Protection Unit or EPU as it was known, which provided Jess with personal security while the legislature was in session. They gave him the Beretta, their standard issue firearm since the Smith and Wesson .357 revolver had become obsolete in the age of well-armed drug lords, as recognition of his expert performance on the firing range at the Patrol's Academy. It was a side of him that surprised them, that of crack shot. Neither they nor he had any idea at the time how important the gift might become one day.

EPU members more or less openly fought to be assigned to a vacancy in Speaker Stevens' detail. He treated them with respect and like the professionals they were and they responded in kind. And after spending every waking hour with them for six months every year, the troopers became like members of his family. No one was sadder with Jess' sudden departure from the state capital than the troopers assigned to him.

Uncharacteristically, he left the house without locking the doors or turning out unused lights. He didn't bother to leave a note for Sacco, either. Jess was single-mindedly intent upon his objective.

As he was backing out of the driveway, Jess didn't hear the phone ring and keep on ringing. It would have saved him much trouble and surprise had he been there to answer it.

CHAPTER SEVENTEEN

Jess didn't think as he drove east on the Springdale Highway and then turned north on Jump Off Joe Road. He didn't let himself think. He was propelled forward by an obsession to reach his objective. It wasn't adrenaline; it was something else that pushed him. An instinct. An instinct to fight back against something he could pursue and confront. And possibly, just possibly, something he could defeat . . . or be defeated by, it didn't matter. But at least it was an honest battle and on some level, he knew it would be cathartic. There was apprehension as he drove. Hell, there was outright fear. But there was no torment, no guilt, no anguish. And there was absolutely no uncertainty.

Jess had never been to the farm before but it was easy enough to find thanks to the large, neat block letters on the mail box. He turned and slowed his car as it twisted down the hill and through the trees and up the long gravel driveway lined by the neatly painted fence. The fence encased an impeccably trimmed lawn almost the size of a small pasture. To the right was a large barn which also appeared as though the painters made regular visits. Jess was struck by the absence of old or rusted machinery that marked so many farms in the area. Everything was in its place.

The driveway ended in a turnaround that created a small island of grass and flowers. Small, painted wood figures decorated this patch and greeted visitors to the old and modest three bedroom rambler at the apex of the driveway. The house was in complete harmony with the rest of the farm, in color and neatness. It was off-white with a blue accent on the window shutters. Jess thought the place looked like a cover photo for *Better Farms and Yards*.

He pulled the car right up in front, got out and strolled to the door as naturally as if he was coming to collect for the month's newspaper subscription. Ringing the doorbell once he stepped back off the front concrete porch. This was something he once taught candidates for the legislature. "People will be more comfortable when they come to the door if you're not right in their face," he instructed. "Don't invade their space." Old habit or not, today he wasn't trying to make anybody feel comfortable and was definitely planning an invasion of "space."

The door opened and the man pushed the screen door forward before looking up and recognizing Jess. Just then, Jess removed the Beretta from his jacket pocket and pointed it at Barney Rubble, award-winning teacher and model citizen. "You and your brother are coming with me, Barney."

Rubble didn't change the expression on his face and said nothing for a minute. He quickly glanced at the Beretta and back into Jess' eyes as though to take a measure of his intent. "Sure, Jess. Tommy's not here but do you mind if I get my coat first?"

Jess stepped forward and kept the door open with his foot while keeping the gun aimed squarely at Rubble's chest.

"Okay," he said evenly, "but first, put your hands behind your head and interlace your fingers." Rubble did as he was told. "Now, tell me where Tommy is."

"He went to Seattle and will be back any time. In fact, I thought he forgot his key and that was him at the door."

"Well, let's just see for sure, Barney. Turn around and move slowly into the house. Keep your hands behind your head at all times. Do you understand me?" Jess was all business.

"Yes, of course." He did as he was told. Jess moved in behind him and quickly surveyed the front room with his eyes, always keeping the gun leveled at Rubble.

"Now, Barney, you are going to take me on a little guided tour of your house. We're going to check every room and every closet. One at a time. Just to make sure your brother isn't here somewhere. You are going to stay ahead of me and move slowly. Are you still understanding me?"

"Yes." Barney proceeded compliantly first into the kitchen, dining room and the utility room end of the house. Then they backtracked to the opposite end of the house where the three bedrooms were and methodically went through them one by one. When they were finished, Jess motioned Rubble back to the living room.

"What are we going to do now?" Barney asked.

"I think we'll wait here for just a while longer and if Tommy doesn't show up in a while, we'll leave. Get down on your knees and keep your hands where they are," he ordered Rubble with a wave of the gun. Jess figured it would be impossible for Rubble to move at him quickly from his knees.

"Oh, c'mon, Jess. I'm too damn old to do anything. Let me sit down for Chrissakes." Rubble seemed more annoyed at the prospect of the discomfort than he did at having a loaded gun pointed in his face.

"Get on your knees. Now!" Jess barked with intensity and Rubble reluctantly dropped to his knees.

"You mind telling me what this is all about? As long as you enter my home at gun point, I think I have a right to know why."

"You know damn well why I'm here. I'm taking in the people who killed Gary Lother, who probably killed Bill Page and who are involved in some kind of drug dealings. Methamphetamine is my bet."

"I see," Rubble responded conversationally. "So, the retired Speaker and teacher has become a law enforcement officer." There was a slight tone of taunting in his voice but nothing overt.

Jess let the jab hang in the air for a moment. "This is personal," he finally explained. At that moment Jess didn't know how personal it would become.

"And what brilliant deduction led you to my doorstep, may I ask?"

Jess ignored him. After a few minutes, Rubble persisted, "Come on, Jess. We're just sitting here with nothing to do. I'm curious. At least tell me why you never believed the Lother boy died accidentally. That was true even after the autopsy report, wasn't it? What did you think you knew?"

Jess sat down on the edge of a chair across from Rubble, never taking his eyes off him and never lowering the gun.

This time, Jess answered. "I knew the Lother kid. I knew he was a great swimmer. I knew he had a lot of common sense. I knew he wouldn't go swimming alone at night. I knew enough."

"Enough to do what?"

Jess paused. "Enough to take it the next step."

"Which was?"

"Break into the Lother house when the family was away. That's when I found the reflux condenser I brought to you at school. Gary had tagged and dated it the day before he died."

"I don't understand why you thought that might mean so much."

"I probably wouldn't have except for a couple of other things. The night I was in the Lother house there was a prowler outside. It was like someone had the same idea at the same time for the same reason."

"People should be more careful, shouldn't they?" Rubble's sarcasm was very near the surface.

"When I went down to Inland Empire Chemical Supply Company the next day, there was a transaction ahead of me that seemed a little curious. I was explaining it to Bill Page the next night when the fire alarm went off and the Lother house was torched."

"Total carelessness on someone's part. Sounds like you poked a stick into a hornet's nest."

Jess looked at him for a moment as though he were trying to understand Rubble's sarcasm.

"Anyway, Page found a vacuum pump under the house in what used to be Gary's bedroom. This one had a tag on it from Inland Empire. The next day, Page went down to Inland Empire and asked some questions about the vacuum pump and the reflux condenser. My guess is he also showed the owner a picture of Gary Lother. And the following day, yesterday, he was killed. You might say it was **your** fatal error, Barney."

"What do you mean?" Nothing about Rubble's composure indicated he had interpreted the statement as an implicit threat.

"After you – or Tommy – murdered Page, I decided to go back down to Inland Empire last night myself. I thought Bill might have learned something that led to his death."

"So?"

"So, I found an invoice for a reflux condenser with Tommy's name on it. I didn't know what to think at first. I even missed it the first time through. But I went back to the invoice because of the last name, **your** last name. I noticed it was your address and I knew you had a brother living with you. Someone told me he was on some kind of military mental disability or something. Delayed stress syndrome, I think. They said you took care of him. Anyway, I thought about how you told me you ordered all your supplies through the catalogue. And how you barely remembered the name of Inland Empire."

"That's not enough to get you out here."

"Right. You didn't know it but before Page was killed yesterday, he shipped the vacuum pump over to the State Patrol's crime lab for analysis. It revealed traces of methamphetamine, a drug produced with the aid of a reflux condenser and a vacuum pump."

"So, you have Tommy's name on an invoice and evidence of drugs somewhere, maybe even made by Gary Lother, and you get in your car and drive here and . . . and do this? Jeessss." He stretched out his enunciation of Jess' name as though he were expressing disapproval.

"Amazing, isn't it, Barney. How I got so far on so little." It was Jess' turn for sarcasm. "But I'm not quite done. I also had the state crime lab take another look at the tissue samples from Gary's autopsy."

"They keep tissue samples? I didn't know that."

"In some cases, they keep them for several months. And it was the tissue samples that brought it all together for me."

Barney smiled an evil grin finally dispensing with any facade of innocence.

"A stupid frog. A stupid goddamn frog," Jess exclaimed.

"Well, in all fairness, Jess, not just **any** stupid goddamn frog. A very special frog. *Phyllobates aurotaenia,* to be exact."

Jess recited the information he received from the governor. "One with a skin extract, *Bachrachotoxin,* so toxic it is used as arrow poison by certain tribes. It requires such minute quantities – a tiny pin doused in it is lethal – that a standard autopsy wouldn't reveal it. Best yet? The death would appear to be drowning to anyone even though you probably killed him before you put him in the water."

"Now, I am impressed, Jess." Barney was mocking him but Jess ignored it.

"I remembered seeing the display of exotic animals from South America in your classroom. It all clicked into place. Your brother's name on the invoice. A chemistry background. A rare animal that you would know about and possibly have. All information led to your door. The only thing not to clear to me is why you murdered Gary." Rubble said nothing. Why did you?"

"Simple. He threatened the operation."

"How does a fifteen year old boy threaten you for God's sake? In any way?"

"You said the boy had a lot of common sense, Jess. But he also had a little too much curiosity." Rubble spared Jess the cliché about the cat.

"Last summer, he was riding his motorcycle in the woods above our barn. Well, the one big problem with meth production is its smell. It's awful. Potent enough and strange enough to grab the attention of even a passerby."

"Gary?"

"Right."

"This smell, it wouldn't happen to be something like cat urine, would it?"

"Exactly." Rubble raised his eyebrow as though he were about to ask Jess how he would know that but changed his mind. "Well, Gary wanders down and sees Tommy and starts asking about the smell, saying it isn't like anything he ever smelled before."

"What happened then?"

"According to Tommy, nothing. Tommy got a little irritated and started yelling at the boy to get away. Anyway, the boy knew it was my place and didn't think he was doing any harm. One thing led to another and the boy took off. But I think he came back a couple of weeks later. I saw someone running off with something. I couldn't be sure but I thought it was the boy. Later we figured it was the vacuum pump we used earlier. The irony is the boy didn't realize what a favor he had done us."

"What do you mean: 'did you a favor'?"

"We decided the smell might present a real danger. After all, it wasn't just nosy fifteen-year old boys who might happen to wander near the farm. So, we decided to take some more precautions. We literally air proofed the back of the barn where we produced the meth and set up a ventilation outlet. We vented the room through a pipe in the ground with charcoal filtration. The outlet ended at our small chicken coop. By the time the odor was filtered and run through the coop, it was bad but not overpowering."

"What about the boy?"

"He came back. In fact, I think he came back more than once although we tried to keep an eye out for him. One day I discovered a reflux condenser was missing. The next day I caught Gary on the property snooping around the barn. I think he was glad it was me and not Tommy because I just pretended like he had come visiting or something. 'Visiting' may not be the right word since the kid didn't talk much. That was one shy kid. Anyway, I asked him to dinner and he finally loosened up a little bit. You know what the kid thought? He thought there was something going on here that I didn't know anything about. He thought that Tommy, who was away that night, was doing something. I knew then that he was not going to leave well enough alone. Imagine that! Imagine a damned kid, a high school student, just like I've given my life to for more than thirty years, about to ruin a great enterprise, my chance to get something great out of life. So, I decided to prepare a very special dessert for him and well, the rest, as they say, is history." He made the last comment with a shrug of the shoulders. "It was easy enough to take Gary's body, unseen, down to Loon Lake in the middle of the night. His parents thought he was sleeping out anyway and wouldn't – didn't – miss him until after the body was found."

"Just like that, huh?" Jess asked. Rubble shrugged his shoulders again. His cold bitterness angered Jess and he tightened his grip on the Beretta. "He 'did . . . you . . . a favor'?"

Rubble rose unexpectedly from the ground and rubbed his knees, sore from supporting his weight on the hardwood floor for so long. Jess, startled, jumped up off the couch and moved a step closer. "What are you do-ing?" he shouted. "Get back down there."

Rubble ignored him and stepped slowly backward, lowering himself into a well-used easy chair, the big, soft comfortable kind used to watch television and doze in, the kind that lean all the way back until they are com-pletely parallel with the floor. "I don't think so, Jess. My knees are killing me."

Rubble spoke casually, seemingly oblivious to the loaded Beretta pointed at his face or the angry man stand-ing over him.

"I've just gotta' sit down here for a while."

Jess towered over him with an increasingly tight grip on the gun. He was perplexed by Rubble's behavior and his suddenly cavalier attitude. Rubble made no threaten-ing gesture, but neither was he responsive to the threat of the weapon.

"I guess in hindsight, maybe I shouldn't have had Tommy burn down the Lother place. Seems like that was kind of an incendiary for the whole affair." He smiled at his own bad pun.

"Oh, well. You can't put the shit back in the cow. Come to think of it, Jess, you did me a favor, too."

Jess tilted his head with curiosity at that odd assertion. He was struggling to maintain his composure. "What did you say?"

"I said you did me a favor by coming here." Rubble was smiling again.

"You mind explaining yourself?"

"Sure. I actually tried to call you earlier. You must have just missed my phone call." Rubble was enjoying this.

"Go on."

"I just wanted to let you know that Tommy and I thought you might like to come out and see Sacco. Tommy's guarding her in the barn right now."

CHAPTER EIGHTEEN

"Ahhh, Jess, I knew you went back down to Inland Empire last night. You tripped the security system on the way out. You didn't know that, did you? Tim called to let us know someone had broken in. Nothing was stolen. It just appeared to him as though someone had gone through the invoice files and it wasn't hard to figure out who that might have been. Poor Tim. He's getting more than he bargained for. He just wanted to sell a few extra chemicals. All legal. As long as no one asked any questions everything was all right."

Rubble spoke with mock concern. "You know, Jess, you've really been a little obsessed with this whole matter. It's really not very healthy."

Jess was numb and it took him a minute to hear Rubble's words. He was still digesting the announcement that Sacco was being held captive out in the barn.

"You're bluffing."

"No, Jess, not really. I am a very careful man, you know. I don't like to leave any 't's' uncrossed or 'i's' undotted. That just wouldn't do. That's why I had the Lother house torched. I didn't know what all the boy had picked up from the property around here. He didn't say. And if anything had fingerprints on it, well, Tommy was in the service and his fingerprints are on file some-where. Who knows what might have led to what. And that was the problem with Page. He actually wasn't that close to finding us but the man was a professional and you never know. I had a lot of respect for him. Healthy respect. No, this is much safer, much more prudent. Don't you agree?"

Jess stepped to the foot of the chair in which Rubble comfortably sat. He pulled the hammer back on the Beretta and put the barrel of the gun right against Rubble's eye. "You're bluffing," he said again. Rubble remained to-tally calm and self-assured.

"No, Jess. I am not. And –" he glanced down at his watch without moving his wrist or his neck – "in exactly 20 minutes you will hear a shot fired from the barn to prove it. That is, if you don't start exercising some com-mon sense."

Jess pushed the gun even harder against Rubble's eye, so much so that it tilted his head back slightly. "What are you saying?"

"I'm simply saying, Jess, that I left instructions with Tommy to shoot and kill Sacco at exactly 5:30 if I did not come out to the barn with you in tow."

"How do I know you actually have her?"

"Oh, Jess, she was easy. As easy as you would have been had you been home to take my call earlier. As easy as it was to get Bill Page off in the woods in the middle of no where.

"I simply waited until I saw her walking to her car this afternoon. I caught up with her and told her about everything, told her we had you out in the barn and told her if she didn't get in her car and drive straight here, we would put a bullet in your brain. Poor woman. She was so shocked she was afraid to call my bluff – it really was a bluff then – and go call the police or call home and see if you were there. No, she came running. Right into the trap. I knew she would. Never doubted it for a moment." Rubble was obviously pleased with himself notwithstanding the Beretta jammed into his eye socket.

Jess remained motionless for a several seconds. "Let's walk." Slowly, he backed off and allowed Rubble to rub his eye and stand up.

"The barn. Go."

Jess was outwardly intense and inwardly frantic as he scrambled to come up with an idea about how to deal with the situation if Rubble was telling him the truth. He didn't mind that Rubble was moving slowly or that he was so full of himself that he started almost babbling with pride.

"The whole thing was quite easy. When you stop and think about it, one only needs five things to become very wealthy at this drug business. I don't touch the stuff myself although I suspect Tommy does on occasion. I have to watch that, though. Meth is highly addictive. I'm not sure why anyone would ever take that shit. It will mess a person up quick, but that's one of its beauties. It becomes addictive very fast. And if they live long enough, you have a built-in customer base. Anyway, as I was saying, it's easy. You need the equipment. We got that at a meat packing plant that closed. A few large vats. A boiler operation and we jury-rigged a refrigeration deal.

"So, you take the equipment and experiment around – that's actually what the vacuum pump and reflux condenser were for – until you have a formula and process that produces high grade product. It was amazingly easy. Really. I've done experiments in high school more complicated than what we've done here. You could probably go down to the local library and get the formula if you were astute enough.

"And distribution was a snap, thanks to Tommy. He

spent several years down in LA after he got back from Vietnam. He fell in with some biker types and made a few friends. Well, they are what **he** would call friends. Anyway, talk about a beautiful distribution system. No fuss, no muss. Just fix up the batch, send Tommy to LA to exchange the product for the cash and, voila', instant millionaire."

Jess winced at the expression. He had been described that way, he was sure. Never to his face but certainly when he wasn't a party to the conversation. It hurt to even think about it and now to hear the expression out loud brought a sharp emotional recoil. Rubble missed the reaction altogether.

Jess forced himself to think about his predicament and what he would do if Sacco really was in the barn. Rubble would gain the advantage and a dangerous circumstance could turn to catastrophe. No immediate solution occurred to him. He decided to apply a lesson from his political life: when no course of action appears obvious, stall like hell. It would not be hard to keep Rubble talking on the way to the barn.

"So, that's only four, isn't it, Barney? Know-how, equipment, materials and distribution? Didn't you say there were five things required to be a successful drug manufacturer, not counting FDA approval?" Jess wondered if light sarcasm would fake Rubble into believing he was less nervous about the situation than he really was.

"Right! Right you are, Jess. I'm glad you asked because I'm really quite proud of the last part." As though he weren't proud of every last damn detail of this deal, Jess thought.

"The last part is in some ways the hardest. You see, you have to clean the cash. You have to find a way to make it legitimate or else when you start spending it, the Federal government might get curious. And the Federal government is fairly insistent upon receiving its take, you know. It's dirty cash that sends a lot of people to jail, not the underlying enterprise."

They were walking down the driveway, and Jess was surveying the big barn off to the left. It was huge – the size of a couple small apartment buildings. Like everything on the farm, it was painted in the same colors, off-white with dark blue trim. The roof was silver aluminum. A large set of sliding doors were closed in front but a regular-sized door stood slightly ajar on the side facing the two men.

"Truthfully, though, I never planned to spend it. At least not here. You see – and I think you will be glad to hear this – Tommy and I are leaving tonight and I'm afraid we won't be coming back. That's really why you and your lovely wife are here, Jess. Just to buy us a little time to leave the country."

They were getting close to the barn and still no plan occurred to Jess. It dawned on him that this had been happening to him a lot lately. "So, Barney, how did you clean the cash?"

"Oh, yeah. Well, first, I bought some small old gold mines. Three of them in different parts of Washington. Each one was near an area where there either had been a lot of gold mining or there had been rumors of possible big finds. Then I sent Tommy to Alaska to meet with an old acquaintance of mine who is a gold miner in the Yukon. The man acted as a broker with a bunch of miners. Every so often, Tommy would go up to Fairbanks and meet with the man and buy gold from him.

"The miners liked it a lot. They were paid a premium price for their gold and it was in cash. Easier for them to escape Uncle Sam's long arms that way, you know. And the broker liked it because he got his take coming and going. Lots of people were getting rich off this deal, Jess."

They were almost to the door and Jess, still without a plan, was becoming more tense and alert for whatever might happen next. "Yeah, and then what?" he asked absently, just trying to keep Rubble preoccupied while his mind continued to race.

"Well, Tommy would fly to Seattle and go to a metal refinery and sell the gold again. He didn't have to report where it came from. Can you believe that? There is no federal requirement to disclose sources of gold? They want you to report everything else. Anyway, in case the refinery ever got suspicious, Tommy would just make references to our several mines. And if the refinery ever got totally suspicious, it could check and find out we really did own three gold mines in Washington, every one being a plausible candidate for large finds.

"Here's the topper, Jess. We simply kept our money on account at the refinery where they offer a money management service for suppliers. The company has the capability to wire the money overseas on a moment's notice – which they received earlier today. Now, fourteen million dollars is waiting for Tommy and me at a distant port of call. It will be a good life. Too bad it took so long to get here."

Jess was still stalling while his mind churned. "Fourteen million, huh? No wonder it took you so long."

"Oh, no, Jess. you misunderstand. It didn't take me that long to accumulate the fourteen million. Less than a year. I just wished I'd have thought of this when I was young enough to enjoy it longer is all.

"Heavens no, it didn't take long. You see, Jess, this is the largest methamphetamine lab in the country. Maybe in the world. We were actually beginning to affect prices world-wide. Or so they tell me. You know, in some places I am known as the 'Speed King'. People who don't even know my name know what I am doing although they don't know where I am doing it or how. I revolutionized the business, Jess. I was to meth production what Henry Ford was to automobiles. I mass produced it. Usually, the stuff is made on a table top or in a kitchen somewhere but I mass produced it for the first time."

Jess was tired of Rubble's bragging and frustrated at not knowing what to do next. His options narrowed as they approached the door and saw Sacco's car sitting in the barn over Rubble's shoulder. Something approximating panic began to fill his stomach.

"Stop!" he ordered Rubble in a loud whisper. "Now, walk very slowly up to the door and push it open."

As they gingerly stepped through the frame of the doorway, Jess surveyed the barn's interior. The barn had a huge concrete floor, clean enough to cook on. And there wasn't much in the way of clutter. No animals and precious little equipment. Straight across the barn from him was a stalled off area with tools neatly stacked on shelves and hung in labeled places. Farther to the left on that wall was a lone all-purpose John Deere tractor which he could see over Sacco's car. And along the wall to his left were the various attachments for the tractor, each suited to a specialized task.

The back wall had two doors. Jess didn't know it but the one on the left, to the larger room, led to the meth lab. The door on the right led to Sacco and Tommy. Above the rooms was a huge loft, presently filled to capacity with hay from the summer.

"Where is she?" Jess asked quietly. His voice echoed slightly in the cavernous space.

"Back door on the right. And now, Jess, I think it's time you gave me the gun."

"Not likely. Not yet, at least." Jess was holding the gun straight out from his chest. Let's go back there first." He waved the gun in the direction of the door with just his wrists. Within a few steps they were even with Sacco's car and Jess told Rubble to wait while he glanced in the front and back seats. Keeping the Beretta on Rubble, he opened the driver's door and flipped the trunk latch and then slowly walked backwards to look inside.

"Jess. Jess. Jess. Enough of this. Why don't you just give me the gun and you can see Sacco. It's really that simple."

"Keep walking."

"Fine, Jess. Whatever you say."

As they walked toward the back, Jess noticed the door on the left was made of a metal with an unusually strong locking system.

"Fort Knox, huh?" Jess kidded.

"Good as gold. Good as gold." Rubble was a pun a minute.

They reached the door and stopped. Rubble extended his palm outward as an invitation to try the door. Jess slowly took hold of the knob and twisted both ways. There was no give.

"Well, Jess, you have" – he looked down at his watch – "exactly four minutes. That is, if Tommy's watch is synchronized with mine. I certainly hope his isn't running a little fast. Could be, you know. That would be a shame. I like your wife, Jess. Really. She's a fine principal and doing a good job with the community and the students and the teachers. Why, I bet she'd even give me an excellent evaluation." Rubble's voice was tinged with some bitterness.

"Let's say that were to happen. Say the appointed hour arrives and there is a shot on the other side of the door. What would keep me from emptying my Beretta into your worthless carcass, Rubble? Why wouldn't I do that?"

"That certainly would be your choice, Jess." Rubble showed no sign of nerves whatsoever. The two men stared at one another for a full minute.

"How do I even know she is in there?"

"That's easy." Rubble stepped to the door and gave a special knock, obviously a prearranged signal. To Jess, it sounded like the "shave and haircut, six bits" rhythm he had been taught in grade school. Everything with Rubble was so carefully planned. "Tommy, take the tape off her mouth." He stepped back and invited Jess to step to the door.

"Sacco. Paisan, this is Jess. Are you in there?" Jess shouted at the door but kept his eyes and Beretta trained on Rubble. "Are you in there, Sacco?"

"I'm here, Jess." Her voice was steady and clearly loud enough to be heard. There was a muffled voice and she added, "I'm fine. I'm not hurt."

Jess and Rubble stared at one another. Rubble kept a "Well? What now?" look on his face and finally looked at his watch. "Two minutes, Jess. It's your call." He held out his hand to take the gun.

Jess thought about shooting Rubble to see what reaction that would bring from the other side of the door, to see if Tommy would keep the schedule or begin negotiations, realizing his life, too, was on the line.

The thought of cold blooded murder chilled him even though he felt Rubble was without redeeming value. He remembered another time when he took other men's lives, men who probably left the world a lesser place he thought, at least compared to this one.

Maybe he could fake shooting Rubble by firing a shot. Then he could break the door down and rush Tommy. Maybe Tommy would be so unnerved by the gunfire that he would be momentarily shocked, caught, like a deer in headlights.

"One minute, Jess," Rubble announced.

Jess looked at the gun and the door and into his soul. He knew Sacco was alive right now. He wasn't sure she would be if he did anything other than what Rubble requested.

He reverted to form and played one last stall. This time, though, the stall meant he turned the Beretta over to Rubble. It gave him a little time. He just wasn't sure how much.

"Good boy," Rubble said smiling as he took the gun and pointed it back at Jess. He gave the special knock on the door again and said, "Open up, Tommy. Everything is under control."

CHAPTER NINETEEN

The door swung open and all Jess saw was Sacco. She sat facing him on an old, wooden, white chair in the middle of the room with her legs bound at mid-calf to the legs of the chair and her hands tied behind her back. A ball of gray wadded up duct tape that had once silenced Sacco now rested on the floor beside her.

Jess rushed over, knelt down and put both arms around her. She had never felt so good to him. He held her tight and kissed her on the cheek and squeezed hard as though his strength might reassure her. Usually, she was the one doing the reassuring.

"Jess," she whispered as she strained to meet his embrace as best as she could with her neck and shoulders.

It was a sterile room, about twenty feet by twenty feet with the same immaculate concrete floor as the outer barn. The walls were the same off-white as everything else on the farm. There were no windows and only a single overhead light bulb, directly over Sacco's head. It was stark in more ways than one.

The only visible use of the room, other than detaining hostages, was to store paint supplies. The entire back wall was a built-in shelf, painted standard off-white, on which there rested gallon after gallon of paint cans, scraping tools, roller pans, brushes, a small sprayer, and rollers.

"It's all right, Sacco. It's all right," Jess whispered back. The look of fear in her eyes was completely foreign to him and was more unsettling than the gun at his back or the seeming hopelessness of the situation.

As he hugged her even harder, she whispered so that only he could hear, "The light, Jess. The light."

"What?" he asked, completely confused.

"The light, Jess. The light," she whispered louder and with some desperation. He looked up at the light bulb trying to make sense of her signal.

Behind him, Jess heard Tommy entreat his brother, "Come on. We have them now. Just like you said. Let's tie them up and go. Let's get out of here." Jess thought Tommy was overly anxious given that he and his brother were the ones holding the guns. He didn't know that Tommy had been nearly two days without his best friend, "Coffeemate."

"Come on, Barney. Let's go!" He sounded a little like a whiny teenager insistent upon leaving for a movie.

Jess turned and put his arm around Sacco so that he could see the two brothers by the door. Tommy was dressed in blue jeans, a dirty tee shirt and an old Army fatigue jacket with his name showing above the left front pocket. The insignia had been ripped off and it was impossible to tell which unit he had been with. Jess noticed a small caliber gun in Tommy's hand, probably a twenty-two. Not much of a weapon, Jess thought. In fact, unless strategically aimed at close range, it wouldn't stop much.

Tommy looked tired and nervous. He was jumpy and his body bounced from side to side as he pressed Barney to depart.

"Soon, little brother, soon," Rubble responded. "Jess, move away from Sacco and get down on your knees and cross your ankles and your fingers behind your head. Now!" His face contorted with malevolence as he relished his control of his former captor.

Jess scooted a couple feet to the side and put his hands behind his head. He failed to interlace his fingers but Rubble paid no heed. Rubble was more interested in the humiliation than he was the security of the position or obedience to the command.

"That's right, Jess. That will be fine. How do your knees feel, by the way? I imagine that concrete is fairly hard. A lot harder than wood even, I bet. Well, just stay there a while and it will get worse." He said it with a breathy chuckle and a mean tone that caused Jess for the first time to consider how stable he was.

"Come on, Barney. Let's get out of here." Tommy's agitation was growing rapidly.

"Sure. Sure, little brother. Just one little detail to take care of. Why don't you go get the car and bring it down? I'll just stay and finish up here and be right out."

Tommy started to leave when Jess spoke up. "What do you have in mind, Rubble? The Gary Lother treatment?" Tommy stopped at the doorway and turned around. Jess continued, "Or is that too subtle this time? No need to be subtle now, is there?"

"Shut up, Stevens. Tommy, get out of here. Go get the car."

"What does he mean 'the Gary Lother treatment' Barney? What is he saying?"

"Nothing, Tommy. Just go get the car. Hurry up and we can leave."

Jess was stunned. He assumed that Tommy knew about and was a part of the murders of Lother and Page. He moved fast to see if any opportunity worth exploiting would present itself.

"Gee, Tommy. Didn't you know about Gary Lother?

He didn't drown like the papers said, Tommy. He was murdered. By your brother here."

"What are you talking about?" Tommy turned to his older brother. "Barney, what is he talking about? Tell me."

"Nothing, Tommy, nothing. Now go get the car and we'll leave. Do as I say, Tommy." Slowly and reluctantly, Tommy started to turn to leave again.

"Tommy," Jess called, "I bet Barney here has a certain collection of animals that he tells you never to go near, doesn't he? Maybe a certain kind of frog. And he tells you to stay away from them at all times because it can be dangerous?" Jess was gambling but there were few other choices. Tommy turned back once again, this time with a look of confusion on his face.

"Well, yeah, he does. Why? What's this about, Barney?" It was Rubble's turn to become agitated as he sensed he was losing control of the situation and his brother.

"Tommy, godamnit. Go get the car!" he yelled.

"Stop yelling at me," Tommy screamed back. "Just tell me what he is saying."

"Listen to me, Tommy," Jess interjected. "Your brother poisoned the Lother boy with secretion from that frog. He had to kill him to get him out of the way because of all the times he came snooping around here. Remember, Tommy? Remember when Gary Lother came around this summer and you chased him off? Remember how some of the equipment started disappearing and how Barney thought it was the Lother boy? Well, he killed him, and Tommy, that makes you an accessory to murder."

"Is that true, Barney?" he said facing his brother. Rubble was trapped and knew it. He also knew that being too directive could prove counterproductive with his temperamental sibling.

"Now, Tommy," he said in a much more conciliating voice, "I didn't want to upset you but the boy could have ruined everything. Everything, Tommy. He could have sent us both to prison for a long, long time. And then all our hopes and dreams would be gone, Tommy. Our freedom. Our money. Everything."

"Ask him about Sheriff Page, Tommy," Jess added quickly, playing his last card. "Ask him about putting a bullet through the head of this county's top law enforcement officer, Tommy. Ask him."

Tommy stared from Jess to Barney with a look of total disbelief on his face. He had gotten home from Seattle late the night before and was not aware of the murder. "Sheriff Page?" he said sounding shocked. "Barney, what happened?"

Rubble was clearly disoriented by this development. It had been a contingency for which he had not fully and carefully planned like he had everything else. "Tommy," he said soothingly, "you don't believe him, do you? I don't know who killed Page but I didn't do it. Why would I do that? He wasn't a threat to us."

"Stop lying to me," Tommy shouted. "I called you and told you the Sheriff had been down at Inland Empire Chemical with the Lother boy's picture. And you killed him, didn't you? Didn't you?"

Jess jumped in. "Tommy, go check his rifle in the house. See if it is still there." Jess kept gambling, this time that the ever-careful Barney would have destroyed or hidden the rifle before leaving town. He was confident that Barney had some way to cover most of his tracks on the way out of town. He hit the bull's eye.

"Shut up, Stevens. I've had just about enough of you."

"Sure, Rubble. And then you're going to kill us just like Gary Lother and Bill Page, huh? That's why you want Tommy to leave. So, you can get rid of us when he's gone.

"Tommy, you thought he was just going to tie us up so you could get out of town forever, right? Wrong,

Tommy. Your brother isn't satisfied with the boy and the Sheriff; he wants to add two more. Is that what you want, Tommy?"

"Barney. No! We can't do this."

"I'm not going to do anything, Tommy. I'm just going to tie Jess up securely so he can't get loose until we are long gone. You're right. There is no need to do anything else at this point." Rubble kept lying as best he could.

Jess was running out of time and knew it. "Tommy, don't believe him! He has to get rid of us. We know everything. Including that he killed the boy and Page. For a drug charge, they may not search the earth looking for you but for killing a sheriff? You'll never be safe. He has to get rid of us and cover his tracks, hoping that people think we were all done in by the same killer. Otherwise, they will never stop looking for you. You'll never be safe, Tommy. They will always be after you." Jess was hammering Tommy with the specter of eternal pursuit, something he instinctively knew would unnerve Tommy.

Rubble walked over and pistol whipped Jess in the face. Jess caught the brunt of the blow on the bridge of his nose. His eyes immediately filled with water as his nose bled on his shirt and dripped to the ground. Jess knew at once that his nose was badly broken. "I said shut up and I meant shut up!" Rubble yelled.

"Look, Tommy," he said immediately turning back to his brother and changing his whole tone of voice. "They had to be removed. But it's all over now. All we have to do is leave. We will have everything we want. No one will know where we went. It's all been arranged. And you don't have to ever go back to LA or to Alaska. You never have to deal with John Baird again. It's all over, Tommy. All we have to do is leave. All you have to do is walk out that door and go get the car."

Tommy was looking from Barney to the couple on

the floor and back again. He seemed to be calming down and Barney pushed on. "I am sorry about Gary Lother and the Sheriff, Tommy. But it's done and nothing can change that now. Nothing can change it now."

Jess heard the words "nothing can change it now" spin around in his head again and again. Faster and faster until he became dizzy and nauseous. At first he thought he was going to pass out but nothing could have been further from the truth.

Sacco said later that she thought she actually heard a snap from inside him. It was a break she had long both feared and hoped for but which never seemed to come. Until now. She knew it would some day. She had prayed it would not do too much damage when it did.

It might have been induced by the pain of the blow. His nose and face were numb for only seconds and then the searing pain arrived. He was bleeding profusely and his face and eyes swelled almost immediately. He had broken his nose once before playing high school football but it had been no where near as painful as this crushing, vicious blow from hard metal. It may have been the catalyst.

Or it may have been hearing Rubble say "nothing can change it." Rubble meant to calm his brother, to seduce him into giving in to the situation, to relinquishing the impulse that what was happening was wrong and needed to be changed. Rubble was applying a small dose of his own narcotic to Tommy, far different from the one in the Coffeemate jar that Tommy took on his own.

But Jess heard something different – something from a different time and place. Jess heard the doctor say to him, "Nothing can change it now." He actually felt the doctor's hand on his shoulder. He saw the doctor's kindly face and saw his lips move as they formed the words, "Nothing can change it now." They may have been the last words Jess actually heard even though they were spoken many months ago.

It was a typical January day at home, gray and lightly raining. Jess sat on the porch in the love seat swing with legislative reports and correspondence from work piled on his lap. He wore blue jeans and a heavy down jacket which allowed him to work and breathe the fresh cold air of the outdoors. He was home from the legislative session for the weekend but that didn't mean the work stopped. It merely meant a slower pace, a pace designed to compromise his proclivity for workaholism with his need to spend time with his wife . . . and son.

The boy was ten years old and unusually close to his father. He didn't resent Jess' absence during the week of legislative sessions – every night they talked long distance on the phone – as much as he yearned for their time together on the weekends. Just being around his dad was enough even if they weren't engaged in the same activity. But they spent plenty of time doing things together notwithstanding the work Jess brought home. Every weekend meant at least one outdoor activity, usually hiking or cross country skiing, and one movie. Then on Sunday nights, they would read to each other. The boy would read for as long as his voice would hold out and then Jess would do the same thing. The boy loved to read but loved the way his dad read even more, so full of intonation and drama.

It was Saturday afternoon and Sacco was in the house cleaning. This was a compromise in their relationship. On weekends during session, she would suspend her expectation of his contribution to the household enterprise and he would be allowed time to work and be with the boy.

He was riding his bike up and down on the street in front of their house in the older neighborhood in which they lived. Every once in a while he would shout a question or command attention to a new skill. Jess never failed to put his work down and give the boy his full attention. It was wisdom he had gained early in life from a friend, an older Black woman who had successfully raised eleven foster children. She received the charges at various ages and in various states of dysfunction. All eleven children had grown up to become part of their own stable, supportive families. Each had a keenly developed sense of personal responsibility and concern for others. The old woman's secret was simple and straightforward. When asked how she did it, she responded, "Whenever any of my children wanted to talk, I wanted to listen."

Jess set his work down as the boy rode past and shouted "Look, Dad," and climbed up on the bicycle seat with his feet. It gave him less ability to steer and direct his bike. Jess was impressed with his son's physical agility in these matters. Like most middle-aged people, he could not remember when such feats were easily accomplished. Each now seemed a major achievement. Jess was always marveling at the boy and thinking how he couldn't do what the boy was doing and forgetting he had done exactly that thirty years earlier.

Traffic was always slow on the tree-lined neighborhood street. Locals were the most frequent travelers and they were invariably slowing down to turn into their driveways. Not so with the late model maroon Honda that came around the corner accelerating as it went. The Honda had unusual custom wheels that were a bright gold and looked like two malevolent eyes staring at Jess and spinning around and around.

At the last second, the boy, still standing atop his bike seat, lost control and swerved in front of the Honda. The impact made a sickening sound, a sound Jess would hear in his mind every day for months to come, and would hear in his sleep. The boy shot forward and upward like a projectile, landing yards away on his head. As he flew, his face was turned toward Jess with a confused look of terror. His lips started to form a word but no sound came out.

Jess could later describe the driver as a young man with the hair shaved on the side of his head but long and curly on top. He wore a large earring in his left lobe, thick and heavy like an industrial key ring. He made no effort to stop or avoid the child. After the collision, he kept going and it was the last time Jess saw either the car or the man inside.

Jess saw the car screech around the corner and had time to leap up and scream the boy's name. The scream was primal. And it was a scream of abject terror, a feeling he had never known, not even in the jungles of a far southeast Asian country when his life was threatened on a daily basis. He had not known fear like this when he thought the firefight would take his life, the time he was wounded and actually believed he saw the shrapnel slow down as it was about to pierce the flesh of his right shoulder. He wasn't as afraid then as he was that afternoon.

The boy was good about wearing his helmet. Dad had modeled that behavior for him on their many bike rides together and the boy was never self-conscious about looking "uncool." Dad was more self-conscious in his helmet but never let on. So the helmet was on and took much of the blow. The boy's face and neck took the rest.

It was probably the helmet that kept the boy alive for the next three days as the best medical care available was given. Jess and Sacco never left his side except to spell one another ever so briefly for eating or going to the bathroom. There was never any thought or discussion given to sleep.

On the fourth day the doctor pressed Jess and Sacco to get some rest before they dropped with exhaustion.

"Nothing can change it now," he said soothingly. "We are doing everything we can. You should get a few hours sleep at least. I will arrange for a spare bed here in the hospital for you. Do that for me and your son, please."

After much discussion and some argument, they relented. Sacco had enough presence of mind to realize she and Jess were bordering on delirious.

They shuffled off to the special room for them holding hands and visiting quietly about nothing, whispering for no reason whatsoever, as though there were people in the bed next to them. They lay down and held each other tight and fell into a fitful sleep. When they awoke the doctor came in immediately and told them their boy had died quietly and peacefully in the night. Jess never forgave himself for not being there, for not holding his son's hand while he slipped from this life to the next one.

He heard it in his head over and over again. "Nothing can change it now. Nothing can change it now." It was the doctor and then it was Rubble. Then it was the doctor again. Back and forth until the two voices were speaking at him in stereo. He heard both their voices at the same time. Louder and louder. He snapped. And then he exploded.

Out came the rage he had denied for months on end. It was a rage he had hidden from, played a kind of cat and mouse game with. Every time it had stuck its head up, he had swatted it back down. Whenever he heard it rumbling, he would tamp it down like he was churning butter or pounding in fence posts. He never let it out. He never admitted it was there. Not to Sacco. Not to anyone, even himself. It had simmered ever since that day last winter when his only child had died. He had put the lid on tight and no air escaped until finally, as Sacco knew would happen eventually, the lid just blew off.

Rubble's back was partially turned to Jess as he continued his soothing seduction of Tommy. But out of the corner of his eye, he saw Jess throw his arms forward, leap to his feet and charge him. He was totally startled at the blurring swiftness with which Jess came toward him. He didn't believe it possible for someone to get up off their knees and cover the distance between Jess and himself in that little time.

The gun in Rubble's hand started firing. The Beretta's trigger was very light and it went off when Rubble instinctively tightened his grip as he spun. The noise was deafening as it completely filled the confined space.

The first bullet harmlessly punctured some of the paint cans on the back shelf. That started a small stream of the ubiquitous off-white paint onto the floor which created a large puddle in a matter of seconds. The second bullet hit Sacco in her lower left leg and she yelped with its impact. It literally spun her whole body and the chair slightly around. The third and last bullet hit Jess in the right arm, right next to the scar from his previous wound. Ordinarily, the force might have thrown him back and down just from the power of its collision. But not today. Jess didn't feel the bullet hit him. It barely slowed his rush; it was as though someone had given a half-hearted tug on his shirt as he ran forward.

Before Rubble could pull the trigger again, Jess had collided with him head on, like a linebacker making a tackle, and rammed him into Tommy. All three fell to the ground into a pile with Jess on top of Rubble and Tommy sprawled on the ground behind them with his head leaning against the wall next to the door. Tommy's hand banged hard against the wall and with it, the twenty-two pistol went flying, only to land at the feet of Sacco who was helpless to pick it up or do anything, tied into the chair as she was. Tommy was completely stunned by the rapid turn of events and terrified at the sound of the gun fire. He continued to lie on the ground, too scared and dazed to move. His eyes and mouth were wide open.

Rubble recovered from his initial shock almost instantly and he somehow managed to hold onto the Beretta even after Jess had driven him to the floor. They lay on the ground, both kicking and thrashing and viciously tearing at one another. Jess had Rubble's gun wrist pinned to the floor while Rubble was alternately beating on Jess' gun shot wound and butting his head into Jess' broken and swollen nose.

Both men were grunting ancient sounds of primitive survival and screaming the screams of hate. Jess' rage and near-insanity, matched by his younger body and good physical conditioning, more than compensated for the loss of his arm as an effective weapon. He slammed Rubble's hand against the unforgiving concrete again and again until the Beretta careened out and off the wall, scooting several feet away. In the melee, it discharged again, the bullet traveling harmlessly through the wall into the barn. Still, Tommy lay, wide-eyed with fright, and watched the two men locked in animal-like combat. Sacco could do nothing but watch and the pain she felt for her husband was far greater than the torn flesh of her leg.

Rubble maneuvered and brought his knee up hard into Jess' groin, the one area of the body where rage did not enable Jess to ignore the excruciating pain. It doubled Jess up and Rubble threw him off with both hands. Rubble quickly looked around as Jess frantically struggled to regain his breath. He saw the twenty-two first and scrambled over to it on his hands and knees. Just as he was reaching for it, Sacco kicked it with her right foot in a small broom-like motion with as much force as her bound legs would allow. The twenty-two scooted out of Rubble's reach and he looked up at her with hatred as he started over to retrieve it. She tried to kick him in the face but her legs could not reach that far.

Rubble dove the last few feet to the gun and landed on it. He turned as fast as he could and pointed it at Jess.

The last thing he saw before he died was Jess lying on the ground pointing the Beretta at him with his left hand and firing it. The bullet hit Rubble in the face before he could pull his trigger.

*   *   *

The room was instantly quiet. The cacophony in the room was immediately replaced with sheer silence and the rapid transition had its own unsettling effect. The strong smell from the gun fire hung in the air.

Jess spun to face Tommy who curled up into a fetal position at once with his hands pleading with Jess not to fire. He broke into huge uncontrollable sobs. Jess kept the Beretta leveled at Tommy with an intensity of purpose.

"Jess? Gumbah, look at me." Sacco was now as frightened about the look in Jess' eyes as she had been for his safety only seconds before.

She did not know the man whose rage had just taken the life of another even if in self-defense. And she desperately wanted to establish communication. "Jess. Please look at me." Jess' gaze remained fixed on Tommy who now wrapped his own arms around himself and repeatedly whimpered over and over, "Please, no. Please."

"Jess. Come untie me, Gumbah. I'm hurt and I need to have this looked at." Sacco was speaking calmly and quietly. Her concern wasn't for herself at all but she thought if she had a chance to reach Jess, it would be an appeal for her welfare and not his own. He hadn't shown much regard for his own safety in the last thirty minutes.

Finally, he very slowly turned his head toward her while keeping his eyes on Tommy. Then, when his head was fully turned, he quickly looked over at Sacco and then back again at Tommy. He repeated this a few times until he became aware of the blood running down Sacco's leg and onto the floor.

He rose to his feet with his stare on Tommy and carefully placed the Beretta in his left pants pocket and gingerly walked to Sacco with his body facing Tommy, his right arm limp at his side. He still had not uttered a word or a sound. When he was even with her, he crouched down next to her leg and with his good arm, lifted the dress material away from her wound. His motion and gestures were still like he was sleep walking. His eyes revealed no evidence of occupancy.

"Jess! Damnit, Jess. Answer me." Sacco was near panic.

Finally, he looked up at her and seemed to focus somewhat. His brow furrowed slightly as he said, "What was that about the light, Sacco? What on earth were you trying to say?"

Sacco let out a huge sigh of relief and then laughed out loud.

"Oh, thank God, thank God, thank God. I love you, Jess. I love you so much."

CHAPTER TWENTY

"What's that?" she asked. "The Wail," he answered.

"What's that?" she repeated.

"Kind of your all-purpose communication call. Mostly for location purposes."

"I see. Well, if I made that sound, would I find out where you are?"

"You're not a loon."

"Is that a detail?"

He looked at her and smiled and reached over and put his hand on top of hers. They were sitting on the second floor deck, ten days after the shoot-out at the Rubble farm. It was early evening in late September and the weather was showing the change of season. Evenings were much cooler. Jess and Sacco faced the lake in their chaise lounges with sweaters on and blankets over their legs. They had already eaten the meal Jess prepared and the dishes were loaded in the dishwasher.

Sacco's left leg sported a hard cast, the vestige of Rubble's misguided bullet. It had hit her bone and required a brief stay at Sacred Heart Hospital in Spokane. Since her arrival home, he had waited on her hand and foot and enjoyed doing it but not quite as much as she did. She would need to stay off her leg another two weeks the doctors told her, and that meant going to work was out of the question. Ordinarily, she would have developed a bad case of cabin fever, but she basked in the attention and the easy presence of Jess. They talked very little but hugged and kissed a lot and discovered acrobatic ways in which to painlessly achieve sexual ecstasy despite the cast and his own shoulder wound which required him to wear a sling.

Jess suddenly laughed out loud. It startled Sacco and she realized she had seen him smile occasionally but never – not once – laugh since last winter. She smiled to herself and gave brief thanks for her blessings.

"What tickles you, Gumbah?"

"Look out there," he said, pointing to the lake. "Look at the loon practicing takeoffs."

"'Practicing takeoffs'? Are you kidding?"

"No. Look." He pointed again to where the loon was fighting the gravity of the water. It was a frantic struggle.

"Loons are built for diving under water and not flying although they travel great distances. Most birds have hollow bones for better flight but loons have solid bones, an adaptation that has made them tremendous divers. Anyway, they just aren't geared for taking off. In fact, they can't take off from land. Hell, they can barely walk on land. It'll take them a full quarter mile flapping their wings and paddling like hell underneath to break loose from the water."

Sacco watched as the loon continued his comic struggle until the water bond was finally broken and only its splash prints were left in the wake. They continued to watch as the loon circled the lake several times and then crash landed back into the water. Both laughed out loud this time.

"It's getting ready to migrate south. Hasn't quite got the landing part down yet," Jess observed. "Never fear, paisan. He – or she – will be back in three years with a mate. It's just time for them to move on to the next stage of their lives." He let the statement hang in the air. Sacco knew he wasn't just talking about loons. She took it as her signal.

"So, how are ya' doing?" she asked. Even after ten days, they had not really talked about all they had been through.

"Awful. Words can't describe it."

"Try me."

"Well, for one thing I am so damned confused I can't think." He seemed very serious.

"Confused?" She often asked these one word questions as a way of getting people to open up.

"Yeah, confused." He decided to make her work.

"Confused how?" She graduated to two word questions.

"Real confused."

She looked at him and caught the gleam. "What the hell are you talking about you big jerk?" She punched him good naturedly in his unwounded arm.

"It's the light, Sacco. I still don't get it."

"Huh?"

"In the barn at the Rubble's. You whispered 'The light, Jess. The light.' Whatever did you mean by that?"

"Oh, **that** light. I just noticed that there were no windows in the room and the door was closed. And I figured if you jumped up and broke the light, it would be pitch black."

"Are you serious? I jump up and break the light, casually untie you and we make our escape? Are you serious? No. Are you **nuts?**"

"Well," she said with mock umbrage, "it was just an idea. It's not as though your brute force machismo deal didn't come with a price tag." She knocked on the cast on her leg.

"But you won't be asking me to run with you in the mornings for a while, will ya'?"

They returned their gaze to the stillness of the lake and the setting sun and let the minutes roll by as lazily as the water lapped at the beach's edge.

She wanted to try again. "Serious?" It was a question seeking permission to deal with potentially painful matters.

"Serious," he responded.

"Do you understand what has been happening?"

"I think so but I'm not sure. Can you help?"

"Sure. Are you ready?"

"Am I?"

"Yes."

"Shoot. Sorry. Bad pun."

"You simply decided to fight back. When Daniel died" – it was the first time either had said his name out loud since they buried him – "you were helpless. You couldn't do anything about it. You had to take it but you didn't accept it. That created a tension in you that grew and grew and grew. As long as you were obsessed with building this house, you were okay. You had an outlet. Functional, but not really coping. Then you finished and started to get restless and then came Gary Lother's death. Your tiny suspicion that his death was not accidental gave you another release for your energy and rage, something to fight back against. An enemy you knew – even though you didn't know. You know what I mean?"

"Even though your explanation was clumsier than a loon landing, yes, paisan, I think I do know what you mean."

"Thank you," he said later. "And while we are on this touchy feely stuff, I have a confession to make. I hope you won't be too upset."

"Yes?"

"I have committed a good size chunk of change without consulting you. I know we have an understanding otherwise but I just didn't want to bother you with it while you were in the hospital. And a decision needed to be made then."

"Go on."

"I visited Tommy Rubble in jail. Seems that he finds himself with no immediate cash on hand. All the available cash, a mere fourteen million dollars, was in the account at metal refinery in Seattle and the DEA has seized it."

"So?"

"So, he is in pretty bad shape and I, uh, well, I told him we would pay for his defense and his drug treatment. Seems he is addicted to methamphetamine. In fact, that day in the barn out there, he was going through withdrawal. He hadn't had a fix in a couple of days and the stress just got to him."

He quickly added, "I'm certain he will be able to pay us back, paisan. The lawyer thinks he's got a pretty good chance and eventually he will inherit the farm and there is value in it but he just needed to get a lawyer on board right away. And so I hired one. For him."

She leaned over and kissed him on the cheek. "You know, Jess Stevens, you **may** be the most wonderful man to whom I am ever married. I think Daniel would approve."

It was a reference to the source of their wealth. Jess had taken out considerable term life insurance on each of them, including Daniel, because the rates available through the state were so low. At the time, they had done it almost as a joke. Because of its source, their money had never brought them real joy. Just the house on the lake and early retirement for Jess.

"**May** be? Just **may** be?"

"Well, yes. Just **may** be. And I don't mind you spending the money at all as long as you don't spend it all. Understood?"

"Understood. Did you have something in mind for

the rest?"

"Well, I have a confession to make, too."

"Yes?"

"College expenses."

"What?" He raised his voice in disbelief. "Sacco, you've got two master's degrees and administrative credentials. What the heck – pardon me for saying this – but what the heck are you going to go back to college for at your age?"

"I didn't say it was for me."

"Well, I'm done, too. So what are you talking about?"

"Well, when I was in the hospital for the gunshot, they kind of, well, they kind of ran some other tests. And, uh, I think we need a college fund."

Jess' jaw went completely slack and a look of total amazement came over his face.

"You're kidding. You're kidding, aren't you?" he finally stammered.

"No, I am not kidding but I think one could find the humor with very little effort."

"My God, I didn't think it was possible," he said. "We had so much trouble conceiving Daniel. We've never practiced – we've never **had** to practice birth control. My God, I can't believe it."

"You need a little mouth to mouth, Gumbah?"

"Jeeez, aren't we too old for this? Aren't **you** too old for this?" His diplomatic skills were in cold storage.

"Hardly, you smooth talker. Hardly. And one more reference to my age and . . ." She mimed a pair of scissors with her fingers. It was the ultimate threat – to cut him off from sexual play.

He didn't hear a word as he sat in stunned silence staring out at the lake. Sacco just smiled and patted his hand periodically to reassure him. She knew when he got over the shock he would be uncontainably happy.

He didn't even notice as two loons took labored flight to head south to find their mates for life and rest on the ocean before returning. The time had come for their lives to move forward.

The phone rang. It was the Governor. This time, he wouldn't take no for an answer.